Deep Water Blues

"Since I was a child, the desolate out islands of the Bahamas have been a home, none more dear than the shark-infested, storm-ravaged, cursed utopia of Rum Cay. . . . *Deep Water Blues* churns with the beauty, desperation, violence, and yearning of those fighting to survive on a speck of land in an eternal sea. As a reader, I am on fire. As a son, I could not be more proud."   —Josh Waitzkin

"Fred Waitzkin effortlessly recreates a singular world with uncanny insight and humor. His language is remarkable for its clarity and simplicity. Yet his themes are profound. This is like sitting by a fire with a master storyteller whose true power is in the realm of imagination and magic."   —Gabriel Byrne

"Loved this book. I could not put it down. A lifetime of memories of my own fishing these same waters."
          —Mark Messier, hockey legend

"*Deep Water Blues* does what all fine literature aspires for—it transports readers to another time and place, in this case, to a sleepy, lush island deep in the Bahamas. Fred Waitzkin writes about life, sex, and violence with aplomb, and Bobby Little is a tragic hero fit for the Greek myths. Hope to see everyone on Rum Cay soon."
          —Matt Gallagher, author of *Youngblood*

"*Deep Water Blues* has the ease and compelling charm of a yarn spun late in the evening, the sun gone down and the shadows gathering in."
          —Colin Barret, author of *Young Skins*

The Dream Merchant

"Waitzkin offers a singular and haunting morality tale, sophisticated, literary and intelligent. Thoroughly entertaining. Deeply imaginative. Highly recommended."   —*Kirkus Reviews*, **starred review**

"Fred Waitzkin took me into a world of risk and violence and salvation that I was loath to relinquish. It's a great novel."
—Sebastian Junger

"*The Dream Merchant* is a masterpiece. A cross between *Death of a Salesman* and *Heart of Darkness*. I believe that in the not-too-distant future we will be referring to Waitzkin's novel as a classic."
—Anita Shreve

Searching for Bobby Fischer

"[A] gem of a book . . . [its] quest is beautifully resolved."
—Christopher Lehmann-Haupt, *The New York Times*

"A vivid, passionate, and disquieting book."
—Martin Amis, *The Times Literary Supplement*

"I've seldom been so captivated by a book."   —Tom Stoppard

"Under the spreading chess-nut tree there have been many chess books. To my mind this is the best."   —Cleveland Amory

Mortal Games

"Waitzkin captures better than anyone—including Kasparov himself in his own memoir—the various sides of this elusive genius."
—*The Observer*

"Compelling." —*GQ*

The Last Marlin

Deep Water Blues

Deep Water Blues

A Novel

Fred Waitzkin

Illustrated by John Mitchell

INTEGRATED MEDIA

NEW YORK

Cover design by Mauricio Díaz

ISBN: 978-1-5040-5774-5

Published in 2019 by Open Road Integrated Media, Inc.
180 Maiden Lane
New York, NY 10038
www.openroadmedia.com

for

Bonnie

Josh

Katya

Desiree

Jack

Charlie

Deep Water Blues

Part I

I've visited Rum Cay many times on my old boat, the *Ebb Tide*, trolled for months of my life off the southeast corner of the remote Bahamian island where the ocean is a rich cobalt blue reminding me of a color my artist mother favored in her abstract canvases. Stella's dark blues were thickly textured like roiling ocean with intimations of agony rising from below like the cries of drowning sailors. My mother hated my fishing life, the legacy of my father, whom she abhorred, but still, I think of her fervent canvases whenever I troll the edges of dark storms, which is often a good place to find wahoo and marlin.

Coming into Rum Cay's south side after fishing, with the sun behind us, the reefs close to the island were natural stepping stones into Bobby's tiny harbor, each of them with a resident population of colorful grouper, snappers, jacks, and crawfish. In calm weather, following the string of reefs marked by red buoys was like a game I played on my way home from school, stepping around one flagstone to the next but never touching. Just that fifteen-minute cruise from the blue water past the reefs into the quaint, dreamy marina was a once-in-a-lifetime experience for me—each time I did it.

Then in the late afternoon, after tying the boat, while the sun was still up, you might be lucky enough to hear the lush singing voice of Flo, the daughter of Rosie, Rasta's ex-girlfriend, who had a little pig farm just outside of town. Flo was a savvy, spirited lady with a love of jazz standards, particularly those of Ella Fitzgerald and Billie Holiday. She played a collection of their music on her little tape recorder while walking the sandy road to work each morning from the village of about sixty souls, while holding hands with her little girl. In the afternoon, Flo took down billowing sheets from a line beside the clubhouse maybe a hundred feet from the feeble docks. Many afternoons I watched and listened as she folded laundry from Bobby's cottages and sang wind-tossed ballads about lost love and regret. Whenever she sang "God Bless the Child" or "Summertime" to her baby, I had to wipe my eyes. All the boat owners looked up when Flo began singing. Then she'd suddenly stop mid-verse to give a hug to her three-year-old daughter who played nearby, next to one of Bobby's fish sculptures, and sometimes the little girl handed her mommy clothespins or stuffed the sweet-smelling sheets into Flo's straw basket.

Many times, I've made the long ocean voyage to Rum Cay to troll off the southeast corner of the island. But my fishing ardor has often been dwarfed by surprises onshore, where breezy sensuous nights plunge me back into the yearnings of a younger man and where I've met maimed and beautiful people on the dock and a few that were evil beyond redemption.

~

In the spring and early summer, the best fishing months in the southern Bahamas, a dozen custom sportfishing boats and several opulent yachts are tied up in the tiny marina, each of them owned by a successful businessperson, usually an older man. In the evening, before dinner, music blasts from big speakers on the boats—a bedlam of sounds—crews exchange marlin shoptalk while carefully washing and chamoising the boats to an immortal glow. As the sky darkens, powerful underwater lights snap on from the stern of each boat showing off an aquarium of sharks, snappers, and tarpon swimming in the harbor. Also, on many of the boats, young women in G-strings and little or nothing else bend over the stern pointing and oohing and aahing at man-eater bull and tiger sharks.

A few ragtag local men from the tiny village have ambled down the dirt road to the dock. They carefully avert eyes from the mostly nude girls while begging for a piece of fish from deckhands who usually keep fish heads and carcasses for the locals, as well as a few whole barracudas. Barracudas are sweet tasting, but one in a thousand is poisonous. Most white men don't eat barracuda, but locals are comfortable with the odds.

Also, tied to the dock with frayed lines, a sailboat, once a graceful sailing sloop, rots in the harbor. Her gear is rusted out, rudder glued in place by a heavy rug of seaweed and barnacles, sails and rigging long since ruined, no lights inside, apparently abandoned; and yet, she's parked alongside this glistening fleet of custom-built yachts like a freakish mutation. Suddenly, a man pokes his head out of the companionway like a diver coming up for air. He breathes the heavy night air, smells the delicious meal drifting from the club, and looks around a little, then he goes back down below. When I look more closely, there is a dim battery light showing from one of the murky portholes. Mike lives inside this relic. From what I can tell, he has no money, lives on rice and scraps of fish and whatever Bobby might bring him from the kitchen. Bobby Little, the owner of the marina told Mike he is welcome to live in the marina forever. FOREVER! Bobby Little always thinks big.

Every couple of years, whenever I manage to visit the island, Mike greets me with a pleasant, casual expression as if he'd just seen me the day before for coffee and Danish. He asks me about my writing and I ask about his. Mike has been writing a novel for years. On one of my last visits to Rum, he read me some pages about a man who lives in a world between the living and the dead. Mike is drawn to the "dead level" as Lawrence Durrell describes the "poor exhausted creatures" he paints so wonderfully. Mike is a steadier writer than I am, always looks beneath the glaze, and doesn't take time off for trolling the southeast corner. I asked Mike when he would finish his book, and his wry expression suggested that my question was absurd.

~

Up on the hill, in the clubhouse, the grand dinner is now winding down. Bobby's guests are stuffed with tuna carpaccio and filet mignon. They sip fine cognac while waiting for Bobby's surprise dessert. His desserts, served at the edge of the deep blue water, are incomparable. Dale Earnhardt holds court at one table with several friends. Mark Messier is on the other side of the room. A guest from one of the other tables comes over to shake hands with "The Captain," and the men exchange a few remarks about this year's prospects for the Rangers. There are about twenty-five people at the tables. They will soon return to their yachts and fish boats as lavish as South Beach condos.

Bobby Little is a short handsome man, deeply tanned from the island life, dressed in an elegant white shirt, slacks, and flip-flops. He walks from table to table, shaking hands, exchanging pleasantries. Bobby is a master chef, a national skateboard champion, a drug smuggler DEA undercover agent, a surfer, expert diver, insatiable lover, acrobatic pilot, world-class archer, raconteur.

Everyone in the room wants a word with Bobby, powerfully built but grown just a little paunchy in his middle years. Passing through the room, he brags graciously or makes fun of his belly—whatever opens doors. He finds time for each guest; but more than that, he insinuates with a smile or a phrase there will be many more island nights like this caressed by soft sea breezes to inspire prodigious feats of love on the grand yachts, sweet dreams of record-setting blue marlin trolled up in the corner. Bobby's Rum Cay nights are memorable as the stars in a perfectly clear Bahamian sky, nights when immortality feels stamped in the bliss of new friendships that will last forever.

In the kitchen, Roderick Smith, known as Rasta, puts the finishing touches on dessert, while talking with a friend, Biggy, who is a small man. Rasta is a huge six-foot-seven with dreads to his feet when he lets his hair down. When he swims in the ocean with his dreadlocks flowing around him, Rasta looks like a giant ancient sea creature.

"You remember Ruby them, over there." He says to Biggy, who nods yes.

Flo nods as well, enjoying Rasta's narration while she washes the dinner plates.

"He had a girlfriend, turn onto me, cause I had a couple

dollars, I had two bikes and things like that, tell her she can live good. We hook up and I start to like her. Tell her she can get a job at the marina. Lots of rich people there, you can make some money just talkin to them nice and things. She stay by me, and we had a good time and stuff like that. She involved with me couple months. Was the beautifulest body I ever had in my life. I been to Cuba and all them places, she had the tightest thingum I ever knew. It was nice, I tell you." Biggy nods gravely.

Flo shakes her head and smirks a little, maybe thinking of her mother and Rasta. She doesn't say anything.

Twenty years ago, Rasta moved to the island from Nassau, looking for a simpler way of life. He lives by himself in a small shack across from Bobby's house on the hill overlooking the marina. Bobby has taught Rasta how to cook and how to make stone sculptures and to operate heavy machinery. Many nights, Rasta works in the kitchen or serves drinks at the bar unless he is feeling too moody to get up from his bed. He understands Bobby's habits and foibles. He loves Bobby and often forgives him.

Rasta has pet Bobby stories, like the morning his friend moved silently through the tall island grass, long hair held in place by a bandanna, and then dropped a wild goat at two hundred yards with his bow and arrow, a feat to test the artistry of Robin Hood. Bobby smiles at Rasta's renderings of his life. Bobby has a keen sense for style, like positioning

Mike's scow in the marina beside the lavish yachts. For sure it amuses him to serve his millionaire guests gamey goat or boar that he shoots with an arrow. One night Bobby served wild goat to Jackie Onassis when she cruised to Rum Cay with her boyfriend Maurice Tempelsman on his yacht. Later that night, Bobby—he was considerably younger then—built a tall bonfire, pulled off his clothes, rolled in the gray clay, and did his famous fire dance at the water's edge with a few of the local guys holding torches and others pounding drums. Absurd though it was, Jackie Onassis was enraptured—everyone was.

"My girl started hanging out in town," says Rasta to Biggy while the giant's hand ladles whipped cream on Bobby's strawberry shortcake. "One night, she come home two o'clock in the morning. Next night, four o'clock. When she wake up, I count out some money for plane ticket, give her five hundred dollar and say I don't want to see you round the house again. She fly to Nassau but come back two weeks later. Rum Cay get in your blood. She get involved with a guy downtown, Marco. He start beating her. Knock out her teeth. Almost choke her to death. Cause she always wearing these little short things."

Flo shoots a look at Rasta. "Shoulda kill him," she says quietly.

"And JJ was grinding her, too. So she went back to Nassau, a changed woman. She get big and fat. No teeth. Every time she see me in Nassau, I always riding some nice rides. She hail me on the road and I stop the car, talk a little, give her couple dollars. She say to me, 'Rasta, that's the biggest mistake I ever made in my life.'"

Biggy nods sadly while Flo stacks the dishes on open shelves.

Bobby wore many hats on the tiny dream haven he was crafting from rock, sand, and bush. He was building new houses for customers and lovely guest cottages for the marina were going up on the dunes above the beach, he and Rasta operating the heavy machinery themselves, the two of them dredging the harbor, pumping fuel for the fishing boats. Rasta managed the dock part of the business, while Bobby was hunting game for the restaurant, carving sculpture from rock and coral, making French cuisine, kite surfing in the bay where he was occasionally chased by a resident hammerhead shark, flying in weekend lovers from Nassau and Miami—time and again falling asleep at the controls but then saving the day. Bobby always saved the day—almost always. So many ladies were thrilled by Bobby, each believing she was the one . . . and she was . . . if only for one night in that bewitching place. There was little time for remorse when each of his two wives took to drink and eventually left him. Bobby didn't seem to mind all that much. It was the way of out island living, he said with a touch of regret. Eventually Bobby flew his wives off the island graciously taking the blame for whatever had gone wrong. He confessed to each of them that the marina was his only real wife.

So many promises made on starry nights. So many best buddies. One night at the bar, he promised Rasta he'd soon become a part owner of the club and marina for all he'd done. Rasta got teary. They both did. *I love you, man. I love you, man.* A big hug. It was so easy to love beneath that clear night sky with a gentle wind from the southeast promising good trolling in the morning.

In the dining room Bobby walks around pouring hundred-dollar glasses of Remy Martin. He doesn't keep track. He winks at one of the old men who has fallen madly in love with his new girlfriend from Colombia. Soon they will walk back to the boat, kissing and fondling even before they climb aboard.

Everyone wants a word or a smile from Bobby. He exchanges pleasant remarks with Dennis, his newest best buddy, who's about Bobby's age and height but fifty pounds heavier. Dennis bought land from Bobby, brought in his own building crew from Miami to put up a trophy house at the far end of the beach. He yearns to be a partner in Bobby's operation. He's already invested money in the marina but wants a bigger share.

Whenever Bobby smiles, Dennis answers with a grin that hints of malice. Word has it, Dennis is a player in Miami real estate with mob connections. Bobby doesn't worry about this. In fact, it turns him on.

While Bobby spreads charm and cognac, two hundred yards away, on the end of the narrow peninsula, across the channel from the marina, a skinny black man pulls himself up on the rocks. He is wearing no clothes. Soon five others struggle to work their way out of the surf, all of them bleeding from rocks covered with crustaceans with edges like razors. The men hear the festive sounds coming from the club. They smell the food. They feel their way along the peninsula of sharp rocks and thistles that runs parallel to Bobby's docks, just across the channel. The men pass the small fleet of fishing boats and yachts and Mike's old sailboat with a dim writing light while Mike carefully revises key paragraphs, grimaces, or nods. Mike's words feel like parts of his body. The men are shivering. The sound of a guitar drifts down from the club.

The six men make their way down the sandbank of the peninsula directly across from the dock. They say a few words and then plunge into the shark-infested channel across from the club. They are not good swimmers. They splash and churn the water attempting to make it across to the festivities on the other side of the canal. The curious sharks are awakened by all the splashing. They swim beneath the crude swimmers, nudge their bleeding legs and feet. One of the men is pulled under. By a miracle, five of them make it across the channel whole.

Bobby's guests are sleepy with food and drink. An older woman notices a tall black man outside, pressed against the window. He is completely naked, his genitals loose and long. Then more naked black men crowd the window. For a moment fear blazes through the room. *Where did they come from? What do they want from us? No clothes.* The Florida women are alarmed. The skinny men are all shivering and hungry and speaking in a strange language, tapping on the window. *Let us in!* The guests are drunk and paralyzed with fear. *Don't let them inside.*

Bobby walks outside to talk to the men, casual as always. One of them speaks a few words of English. They had sailed here from Haiti. Their boat hit a reef some distance southeast of the marina. These men were able to swim to shore. There are others on the boat.

How many others? Ten? Thirty?

They all speak at once. He can't make out what the men are saying.

The party night is over. The older men hobbled back down the hill to their boats with their girls lagging behind. Sadly, the festive mood was broken, the moment of love lost in unwelcome diversion.

No dim light showing from Mike's porthole. *Too bad.* He would have had his own inimitable take on the evening. He would have located the ironies, smelled death with his trademark ardor and sadness. *Too bad.*

One of the captains pointed to the full moon. For marlin fishermen, the full moon presages great action in the morning and for the next several days. "It'll be hot fishing in the corner tomorrow," one of the captains commented. Sometimes when the fishing is hot in the southeast corner, the boats can catch three or four blue marlin in one day.

~

Bobby threw two extra lines and a few life preservers into his beat-up skiff. He asked Dennis to follow in his tricked-out Boston Whaler. Bobby knew his new friend couldn't resist. He'd want to be part of the action. Dennis coveted glory and power but mostly he wanted to be Bobby. Bobby knew this and it didn't bother him—just another part of the circus of his life.

They each took two of the Haitian men and jumped into their boats, cranked the engines, and headed into the night. It was exciting.

Bobby led the way heading east, running parallel to the reef, dodging coral heads, easy going with a full moon showing the way. Bobby knew the reef like his childhood backyard in Miami—he'd been spearfishing this stretch of water for nearly forty years. He followed the broken ribbon of reef for about two miles before spotting a man in a life jacket, drifting in the current. The man was babbling to himself. They eased up to the fellow and his friends pulled him into the skiff.

No sign of anyone else. They moved ahead, slowly following the reef that showed clearly beneath the water. Bobby stopped again. He turned off his outboard, called over to Dennis to do the same. They drifted, listening to the surf breaking on the outer reef. The man pulled from the sea was muttering and shivering. Someone threw a towel his way.

Now clouds were shutting down the moon.

Bobby called to the men in his boat, "Start yelling. Yell!"

"Yell!" he called to Dennis in the other boat. Dennis had an impatient expression. He didn't want to yell.

The men were yelling in a mix of languages. They yelled into a building breeze. It felt hopeless. They listened to the wind. The man in the skiff mumbled to himself.

"Let's go back in," Dennis called decisively to Bobby.

Bobby started the outboard, edged his skiff ahead into the blackness. Now there was something—people chanting, like music, unless it was the wind. No, people were calling. It was pitch dark, the moon fallen behind clouds.

He edged his skiff ahead.

In the other boat, Dennis was nervous as a cat. He didn't want to break up his new boat on a coral head.

There was something in the distance rising from the mist and first spatterings of rain. Bobby drew closer, hit it with a flashlight. The ancient sailing vessel was floating upside down, her bottom splattered gaily with different colored dabs and dots and squares of blues, oranges, grays, and yellows—her waterline had thick rectangles of lighter blue, as if a street artist had created an abstraction to celebrate the triumphant escape from Haiti.

Bobby understood in a glance. The Haitian boat had plowed into the reef and passengers panicked, ran to one side, and the old boat rolled over spilling everyone into the sea. *How many people?* No telling. *Where were they all?*

There were several men and a woman standing on a nearby coral head, calling out. One man was floating nearby with his two palms upturned, an orange life preserver barely keeping his face above water. As Bobby edged closer, he could see the ones on the reef were torn up and bleeding from the coral. And to the east there were more clusters of reef, and he could make out dark shapes trying to hold on to the sharp coral heads. Had to get to them quickly or many would drown or be eaten by sharks.

"One at a time, swim to me," he called out to the people on the pinnacle of coral. They didn't understand or care. Three of them jumped into the water reaching for the skiff that was now rising and falling in a building sea. The one wearing the life preserver remained bobbing in place. Bobby knew he was dead. One of the swimmers was pulling along a teenage girl. He tried to hand her up to Bobby, but the skiff fell away in the surge and the girl sank like a rock. She was gone.

Watching from the other boat, Dennis was shocked. He made a gesture with his arms, nothing to do, and turned away from the Haitians trying to claw themselves into Bobby's skiff.

Bobby pushed men aside getting to the bow. He was wearing his flip-flops, slacks, and white shirt, and holding a mag light. He jumped over, grabbed some air and dove. Down, down, shining the light all over. It was murky. He had no mask or fins. Had to get to the bottom. *Where was she? Down, down. Couldn't find her.* He turned around, swam back toward the coral head. Couldn't see much except the light caught the shape of a few sharks, big sharks. They were looking around. Not hunting. Not yet. Then suddenly, he kicked something with his shoe. Kicked her in the head. She wasn't moving at all. Floating near the bottom. Probably dead. He grabbed her by the hair and kicked for the surface. She was like pulling up a big dead fish. Bobby was way out of breath, but he held on and finally broke the surface with the girl. Got her head out of the water. He grabbed a breath, yelled for his boat, which eased closer. His arms across her naked chest. Finally, the boat was alongside and he pushed her up feeling her swollen belly and pubic hair slide across his face. The girl was about to give birth. She gasped. She was alive.

Bobby was treading water, still trying to catch his breath and could feel something clawing at his back. He managed to turn around, one of the other men from the reef was trying to climb up his back. Bobby shouted at one of the Haitians in the boat to tell this guy to let go. But no one was listening. Bobby managed to twist around and he punched the guy in the face, hard as he could. Punched him again. Then he spun the man around and dragged him to the boat.

Bobby got back to his boat, retching. Took some breaths, then he headed for the next clump of coral, collecting people. Dennis in the newer skiff began doing the same thing. By now, a bigger boat had come out of the marina and was standing by just offshore of the reef. From time to time they transferred Haitians onto the larger boat. The two skiffs pulled scores of people off the coral heads until there was no one left they could see.

"Nothing more here," Dennis called to Bobby.

Bobby was deciding. Dennis wanted to get back to his big boat at the marina, have a drink.

Bobby eased the skiff back to the Haitian sailboat. He pulled up alongside the blue hull, looked around. No one here he could see.

Dennis gestured impatiently, "Let's go, come on." Dennis was finished with this adventure, wanted to tell captains at the dock what he'd done. He would have run back himself but didn't know his way through the maze of coral heads in the dark.

Bobby didn't notice or care. He dove back in, swam to the capsized Haitian boat. He climbed onto the slimy bottom and began pounding on the hull. Pounded some more with his fist. Then a sound from inside. Someone signaling back. People were still alive in there. Some trapped air was keeping people alive. But not for much longer.

Bobby called to Dennis to dive in and help. "Come on, bring a knife!"

Dennis shook his head like a sulking kid. The Haitian boat was a mess of ruined sails, tangled ropes, clothing, floating luggage, soggy mattresses. A swimmer could easily get caught in the debris. There were sharks spinning right below the surface. Dennis shook his head. Dennis had big plans for his life.

Bobby swam back to his skiff, grabbed a rusty filet knife,

and swam back to the Haitian boat. He began cutting lines, clearing away sails, thrashing and cutting like a crazed man.

Then back to the skiff again. He quickly rigged a bridle using a long anchor line. Hardly any time left. Again he called to Dennis. Dennis was a strong swimmer. He needed Dennis to dive in, secure two ends of the bridle to the far side of the Haitian boat. Then Bobby would push his boat into gear and try to flip the sailboat back onto her bottom. It was a delicate maneuver. If he pulled too hard with the skiff, the Haitian boat would keep rolling and end up back with her keel in the air.

"Please, man. Just connect the lines," he called to Dennis. "It's easy."

Dennis shook his head, *No*.

No time. Probably they were already dead. He needed to secure the bridle end of the line to the far side of the flipped vessel, then gun his skiff, try to flip her. He tried to explain to the Haitian captain what was necessary. "Gun her when I wave to you."

Did he understand?

Bobby swam back to the Haitian boat, attached the bridle ends to wooden cleats on the far side of the hull. Then he signaled the Haitian.

Bobby treaded water, watching. Slowly, very slowly, the boat rolled back onto her bottom. Bobby signaled with his hands, and the Haitian backed off on the throttle. Almost immediately a surge of old mattresses, clothing, suitcases, food, regurgitated from a square window at the top of the companionway. Now the sailboat was upright, but she was nearly filled with water and the window and passageway were three or four feet below the surface.

Bobby could see sharks moving below, jerking this way and that, diving into the companionway. They were starting to feed. One of them came at Bobby's feet and he kicked it away. Wasn't much time left. Not with the sharks like this. Not with the boat flipped and filled with ocean. He needed to get inside and see if anyone was still alive. If the Haitian pulled the skiff with too much power, the forty-footer would flip again and roll on top of him. He'd be trapped.

Bobby dove into the hole, squinting, couldn't see a thing. Should have brought a mask. Almost immediately he could feel hands reaching up to him. He grabbed arms, hands, maybe it was two people. He tried to jerk them both out. But the hole was too small. The three of them were wedged into the hole along with mattresses and suitcases. It wasn't wide enough. Out of breath. Bobby had to free one of his hands. He tried to push one of the arms back down into the hole—shoved the guy back down. A little wiggle room. Then with two hands he grabbed a head. He wrenched it up through all the debris. The two of them came bursting through that jammed up hole like a forced birth. It was a kid, terrified. Soon as they hit the surface he was on Bobby's back like a monkey, biting Bobby on the shoulder. Madness crawling, scratching his back and head. Bobby dove back down to the companionway to grab the other person's arm or head but the man or woman had drifted deeper into the hole and Bobby couldn't reach him. He or she was gone. On the surface the kid was again latched on Bobby's shoulders and no one was helping. It took him more than a minute to shake the kid and get him to the skiff.

Bobby went back to the hole again, pulled out duffel bags and more mattresses. He dove into the cabin. Now he could feel arms, hands reaching up to him from the cabin floor, lots of people. They were all dead. They were drowned. Bobby didn't try to pull any more of them out.

~

Back at the marina there was much commotion and suffering. Seventy-six Haitian men and women meandered the dock wailing for the dead, many beseeching women with arms reaching to the cloudy sky, some wore tattered clothes, some naked. Many of the survivors were young. Most of the older ones had drowned.

All this anguish must have wakened Mike on the old sailboat. That's my hunch although I'm not certain about this. How could he have slept through it all? It's my guess Mike stole a glance from his companionway and then went back to his bunk, tried to pretend it was a dream. I couldn't have blamed him. He had his work and little else. There are catastrophes that trivialize any fictive rendering, no matter how brave or dark, no matter the investment in years or energy.

Bobby put out a couple of hoses so the survivors could rinse off. Boat owners offered them towels and food. Bobby brought armfuls of clothing from his house on the hill, tried to get something for each of them to wear while Flo brought food from the kitchen. Many of the younger Haitians ran off and hid Bobby's underwear or shorts in the bushes, then came back to the dock naked again, begging for clothes. The fourteen-year-old kid he pulled out of the boat asked Bobby for his Rolex.

Boat owners and their guests watched from the cockpits of the sportfishing boats.

Eventually Bobby got everyone to sleep on the floor of his clubhouse dining room.

Bobby and Dennis didn't speak again that night. After this, their friendship became chilly and then much worse than that.

The following morning Bobby had to go out to the reef again to recover bodies. Another diver came to help and one of the local guys ran the old skiff.

It was a beautiful day, a pleasant southeast breeze with a two-foot chop on the ocean, perfect for trolling. Several miles to the east, Bobby could see a half dozen boats trolling the corner for marlin.

The Haitian boat was easy to find in the morning light. She was still right side up, now gently hovering five or six feet beneath the surface. From the skiff they could see bodies littering the bottom, beginning to float with their arms reaching up.

Bobby dove down about twenty feet to the bottom, looked around. The bodies were all naked and their skin was falling off. Some were partially eaten. They were all oozing blood from the nose, mouth, and eyes. He took one woman by the hand and began kicking for the surface. Her body was rigid, making it hard to drag her up. Bobby watched the Bahamian guy pull her into the skiff. Salt water and blood was pouring out of her everywhere. The guy became sick to his stomach.

They worked at it for hours. When there were eight or nine in the skiff, they ran them back to the marina where the truck was waiting. Then they hosed the blood out of the skiff and went back for more bodies.

Bobby was dragging a young boy to the surface when the other diver grabbed his shoulder. A sixteen-foot tiger shark was coming right at them, shaking its massive head and biting at the water. Bobby shoved the dead boy toward the shark and both divers swam for the skiff.

All and all, they collected twenty-six bodies. There is no telling exactly how many died from the capsized boat. For days after, half-eaten bodies were washing up on Sandy Point.

The local Bahamians considered Haitians inferior and wouldn't allow the victims to be buried in the local cemetery. They considered it a desecration.

Bobby had to bury them himself. He took his tractor to a

swampy area on the north end of the island and dug a pit. He covered the bodies with lime and filled in the mass grave.

Sometime later, I asked Bobby if this horrible event had taken a personal toll. "No, it never haunted me," he said. "Never even dream about it. I've been around a lot of dead people."

Part II

Time is passing in a manner I cannot grasp. Am I old or young? Is my balance still good enough to make it to the bow of the old boat in a six-foot breaking sea? Some days I feel quite young—especially when I'm trolling lures in a gentle ocean with my wife, son, and daughter headed for Rum Cay. But on this trip my beloved crew couldn't make it, and I'm trolling to the island with elderly and inexperienced friends.

What will I find in the marina Bobby spent decades hammering together with mismatched boards? Will the fancy fish boats cram his rickety docks with music blaring and trophy girls quickening the hearts of older men? Sure, the island has suffered setbacks, but Bobby promised to make it right again, soon the little marina will be better than ever—he said that to me when I dropped him a note on Facebook. And I believe him. Bobby is an unusual salesman, like my dad who had the ardor to close a big deal with his dying breaths.

Maybe (but I'm not sure about this) I traveled to Rum Cay the first time with my father, on his boat, also called the *Ebb Tide*, same as my own boat. I can see Abe Waitzkin clear as day, emaciated, sickly, walking the warped docks, smiling, on his way to the little bar up the hill for a J&B on the rocks. He stops to catch his breath. He looks down into the clear shallow water beneath the sun-bleached planks and sees several bull and tiger sharks—man-eaters—milling around the pilings. He soundlessly makes the word *wow* with his lips. A big Lab retriever resembling Bobby Little's dog, Marlin, ambles to the water's edge, nearby, where the dock gives way to a tiny stretch of sand. The dog barks at the sharks in the shallow water, slaps the water with his paw. The sharks snap at his paws and one throws itself up on the sand trying to get him, but the dog is too fast. The heavy shark wriggles and heaves its way back into the tiny harbor of man-eaters. Abe Waitzkin shakes his head in awe and then continues his slow walk up the hill to the clubhouse. He needs a drink.

This happened many years ago, if it happened at all. When I think of my dad, whom I adored, history and dreams become a seamless narrative. Now, as we leave Cat Island astern heading for Rum Cay, I envision Bobby and Abe walking the docks together.

But how many more times will I be able to make this pilgrimage? I try to blot out this uncomfortable thought.

My friends Doron and Jimmy are sitting with me on the bridge.

James Rolle, seventy-five, has lived his entire life on tiny Bimini Island, three hundred miles to the northwest. When he was a young man, he was a stellar fisherman, ran a twenty-eight-footer out of Bimini for marlin and bluefin tuna. In the evenings, he rode a big Harley, the only one on the island, up and down the entire three-mile length of the Queen's Highway, nodding to passersby like a king watching over his domain of sand, mangroves, and Australian pines, a few shacks on the hill. But now, and for the past thirty-five years, my friend spends his day weighing a couple of potatoes, onions, or chicken wings, or he sells soda or candy to kids. Jim and his wife operate a dusty grocery store about the size of a schoolroom, which is attached to his house on the hill. Jim is overweight and has bad knees. I worry he'll fall and ruin himself whenever he tries to climb down the ladder to the cockpit. Jim is staring out to sea, lost in thought.

Doron Katzman is tall, with heavily lidded crystal blue eyes and bushy gray eyebrows that seem to have a life of their own. He has a ruddy complexion and thick wiry gray hair. In his early twenties, Doron built a catamaran from scratch, and then, with little boating or navigational knowledge and few supplies beside gumption and tenacity, Doron and a fellow youthful lunatic left Israel and sailed the Mediterranean. Soon after, he sailed a small boat across the Atlantic. Doron is a sensitive, understated man, a master carpenter and lifelong sailing enthusiast who lives with his family on Martha's Vineyard.

Doron has traveled with me a few times on the *Ebb Tide* and has fallen in love with blue-water fishing. His newly discovered passion for trolling rekindles my own. Whenever he's on the boat, I want to get one for him. I don't want to let him down.

For the first minutes of a troll, I'm all nerves, watching and wishing for the sight of a tall fin or a slashing bill ripping across the wake. But soon enough, I settle down and focus on the lures skipping, surfing, occasionally plunging into the white water behind the wake as we head toward Conception Island, where we'll anchor for the night. Watching the lures follow the boat feels so familiar and comfortable, like focusing on the breath. I fall deeply into the plunge and dip of the lures—want to watch them forever. I've been enacting this meditation, focused on this same splash, dip, and dive since I was fourteen or fifteen years old fishing with my dad.

I can feel Doron beside me falling into the rhythm of the troll.

And then I glimpse, I think I see an enormous dark shape rising beneath the waves and I start to shriek, "MARLIN. MARLIN. MARLIN!!!" Cannot contain myself.

I stare closely. Seconds pass. More seconds. I don't see anything besides water and skipping lures. There must be a marlin. Must be a marlin!

But only rough seas and my steadfast lures. I'm embarrassed. Why the hell did I yell "marlin" like a greenhorn. I'm the captain.

John is staring up at me from the cockpit. *What? What?* He's scanning the horizon for marlin as if they fly into the sky like birds.

I met John Mitchell on a plane back from California seven years ago. He was sitting beside the window, drawing and writing tiny detailed notes in a fancy black drawing book. I was seated beside him. For hours he never looked up from his pages, and his concentration was such that I found it unsettling. It took all of my self-control not to grab the book away from him and delve into those pages. Finally, I asked him what the hell he was writing about, and he looked as if I'd pulled him out of a two-week meditation. Then we began talking and very quickly discovered a friendship that has deepened over time.

John is a great painter but never fished before. He came along on this trip to draw, etch, or paint whatever we find on Rum Cay.

"I don't see any fish," Doron remarks dourly.

I don't answer. I stare intently at the lures as if there still might be a fish lurking nearby although I know it was just my eyes playing tricks. How can I explain this? The fish in my head—the ones I caught in my youth with my dad and later on with my wife and kids and the ones that I read about in books by Hemingway and Zane Grey—have replaced the fish that have mostly disappeared from these waters. A lot of my fishing life takes place in my head.

"I'm sure we'll catch a marlin today. I feel it," I say to Doron, who nods.

It's true. I feel it.

"Maybe," Doron answers, his Israeli accent filled with merry skepticism while he watches the lures. "Freddy, you always feel it. Every day you feel it. We didn't catch one in two weeks fishing last summer, not one."

"Is that right?"

"Not one."

And yet my mind is filled with marlin and tuna as we troll south—so many memories of great game fish—a picnic of marlin in my head.

It's a windy overcast day pushing into a four-foot head sea. In the horizon, the gray ocean and sky are indistinguishable. I look at the GPS, adjust the course. Usually on these trips, my wife is the navigator. She always knows exactly where we are. She knows which knobs to turn to get the answers. She constantly recalibrates the course while I stare at the lures and dream. Electronics make me nervous but I'm beginning to get the hang of the GPS. I better or we'll never find Rum Cay.

"Hey, Jim," I say, "When you were a charter skipper, you traveled to all the islands, right?"

He nods yes. Jim has a sullen expression. He doesn't want to talk.

"Just using a compass? No electronics, right?"

"When I started fishing, I had no compass, Fred," he says impatiently.

"Come on, Jim."

"I tell you, I had no compass."

"How'd you do it then? How'd you find your way?"

"I just did it. Just used my eyes. We all did it in those days."

"How'd you do it, Jim? How could you travel from Bimini to Cat Island without a compass?"

"Just followed the white line."

"The white line? What white line?"

"The white line in the ocean, Fred. That's how I found my way."

It seems to me with age Jim has become more inscrutable. He unnerves me when he gets this way—when I can't reach him.

Despite myself, I look for the white line in the ocean. Jim stares ahead of the boat, perhaps lost in memories of old fishing days. But more likely, he's worrying about the tiny grocery store on the hill on Bimini. These days the shop, run mostly by his wife, is often out of potatoes or onions, and Jim doesn't have the money to order produce from the States.

Many afternoons, Jim and I have sat on milk crates in front of the empty shop, Jim slapping mosquitoes and sand fleas, which for some reason leave me alone. He glances up or down the dusty road a baseball's throw from the Gulf Stream, and he shares observations about neighbors or friends we have both known for fifty years.

"The world down the road has gotten much harder," he said to me recently.

"What do you mean, Jim?"

"You have one problem and the next day you have one that's worse. One day you feel like I can do it tomorrow. And then tomorrow, you feel like you can do it tomorrow. But tomorrow never come."

I love this crew, but also they make me uneasy. No one can handle the twin diesel boat in a tight spot but me. None of these guys knows how to handle a four-hundred-pound fish beside the boat but me. Of course Jim could do it, but that was a lifetime ago. No one can navigate but me, and I'm not a good navigator. There are challenges ahead. I want to make it to Rum Cay, but also I want to get there and make it home with my crew intact.

Despite myself, I look for the white line. I couldn't spot it, but the chart plotter guided us right into the enchanting Half Moon Harbor of Conception Island, a Bahamian national park, where no fish or shellfish may be caught. The sun came out. The water in the protected lee of the island was perfectly clear. From the bridge, I could see crawfish and grouper on the bottom.

We dropped anchor behind the highest part of the island in about twenty feet of water. I've spent many nights here over the years. There were no other boats. The wind was blowing twenty or maybe a little more, but protected by the bluff there was hardly any wind at all. We were safe from the weather here. Made me feel like a kid in a favorite hiding spot. All this largesse was ours. It was about 5:00 p.m. We were all hot and ready to dive in.

Doron went in first, took a few languid strokes and then sprinted back to the ladder hanging off the stern. He claimed a shark chased him back to the boat. These guys kill me. They can't tell a shark from a grouper. And Jim with his white line in the water. What a crew! I pulled on my trunks and dipped a foot in off the stern—warm as a bath. I dropped over the side, snorkeled nearby. Gorgeous here, heaven. There were crawfish right beneath the transom. I flipped onto my back, closed my eyes, felt the sun on my face. I was thinking about having a beer and a great dinner later with my friends. Then I heard John calling, "Shark, shark." I tried to tune him out, but he kept shouting, "Shark, shark." When I flipped over and looked down, there was a two-hundred-pound lemon shark racing up at my feet mouth open. Before I could move, the shark had my flipper in its teeth and was shaking its head—thankfully, missed the foot, but it pulled off the flipper. I sprinted for the stern ladder. Doron was imploring for me to get in the boat. I was trying. Missed the bottom rung of the ladder with my one flippered foot. The shark was coming at me again. I grabbed the ladder while kicking its head with my one flipper. Doron was now leaning over the side with a lobster spear jabbing the shark in the back while I climbed out.

I made it into the boat in one piece. For some reason, these sharks had it in for us. Five or six of them circled the *Ebb Tide*, waiting. I've been cruising these waters for half a century, and this had never happened before.

Doron made us a great dinner of ribs, rice with corn, a salad, but I couldn't get the sharks out of my head. I've seen many sharks in these waters—often snorkeled with them—but I have never been attacked before. I thought about the Haitian boat off Rum Cay and the half-eaten bodies lying on the bottom. Could the sharks have developed a taste? Or maybe there just aren't so many fish around here to eat.

After dinner, Jimmy had settled into an old swivel armchair by the door, his favorite spot on the *Ebb Tide*. Over the years, I've often asked him to tell me stories of the islands. Usually Jim insists, "Fred, I have no story to tell," but then I pester and coax him. Jim has an unusual narrative gift. He can make a walk down the dirt road across from his store come alive with pathos or humor or dread.

"Tell us a story about sharks," asked Doron.

Jim didn't answer. Across from him in a tattered chair sat John Mitchell with his drawing pad. John was almost always drawing one of us. At the beginning of our trip, modeling for him felt awkward, but after a couple of days, his work seemed to heighten the stakes of a moment.

Jim had a stern, impenetrable expression, as if he resented the imposition of our company.

Then, as if a window had opened, he was suddenly back a half century on the flying bridge of his twenty-eight-footer pulling into Weech's Dock on Bimini, with a four-hundred-pound blue marlin lying in the cockpit, its blackened head draped over the transom. Jim was a powerfully built twenty-two-year-old man who believed that nothing in this world could stop him.

"So we get back from the morning fishing trip, there was three guys waitin to talk. They want me to carry em down to Cat Cay, ten miles to the south. I was happy to go. It was May, which is tuna time, and lots of Bimini fellas down there fishin on the boats for giant bluefin. My good buddy Bradford Banes was mate on one of the boats. Banes was a great fun-loving man. He'd been away fishin for two, three weeks, and I miss hangin out with him in the evenings.

"These fellas wanna troll to Cat Cay and stay there couple hours, have dinner with one of the rich homeowners they knew, and ride back.

"'What you charge us, Cap?'

"'Two fifty for the day and an extra one fifty because I'll have to bring you back in the night.' I was on a roll. I coulda charge em anything. Things breakin my way. I already catch a marlin and made a day's pay. I want to go down to Cat Cay to see Banes and these guys payin me four hundred dollars to do it.

"We troll down and watch this pretty sunset peekin through some clouds that was makin up in the west. We catch another marlin and turn it loose."

Jim turned to me.

"Fred, there was so much fish back then. Not like now. I tell you, guys down in Cat Cay was killin giant tuna. Boats catchin five, six fish in one day—six, seven-hundred pounders. But they lost many more than they catch. Big schools of sharks always trailing the tuna. Often we'd hook a big tuna and before we reel it to the boat the fish half eaten. It was bloody out there I tell you. A man couldn't survive a minute in the water round those tuna and shark.

"Anyhow, Banes was waiting for me when we get into the marina. 'Jimmy, look to the west, man. For sure, big storm comin at us. You can't go home tonight, man. Weather bad.'

"We could already hear thunder and sky in the west lit up with fireworks. Banes right. We'd have to sleep on the boat and try going back to Bimini in the morning. So Banes and I went down to Lewistown. That's what they call black town on Cat Cay. All the mates was there and some good-lookin Bimini girls that work in the houses of rich white folks. We shoot pool and whatever else goes on in the bar down there. Banes telling his jokes. I love that guy.

"Around eight thirty I say, 'Let's go back to the boat case my people come down and I'll tell em we ain't goin back tonight.'

"'No way, not tonight,' says Banes looking at the lightnin to the west.

"But we get to the dock, the three white guys already waitin and they want to go back to Bimini. They don't know nuthin about storms at sea. Banes was nervous, I tell you. He says, 'Jimmy if my mommy was laid out on Bimini this night, I wouldn't go out there in that storm. Look at the fire in the sky, man.' It was true. Lightnin just explodin on the water. Banes was begging me not to go like he knew something terrible gonna happen. And I should've listened, would have change a whole lot.

"But I was a young man and believe nothin bad could happen to me. I thought I could walk on water, Fred. All the older fellas with years on the sea were frighten and tellin me not to go. I guess that also gave me a push to do it.

"'I'll give it a try,' I say to the fellas. 'I think I can make it.'

"'Oh no, Jimmy. Not tonight.' That was the last thing Banes say to me. When you young you just do stupid things. I was gonna show these fellas."

Jim paused a moment. The three of us stood up as if we were thinking the same thing and walked outside to the stern of the *Ebb Tide*. We were all curious to take a look. I snapped on the underwater lights on the transom. There were the sharks, five or six of them, patiently circling the boat. Waiting.

Jim never moved from his chair.

As soon as we were back settled inside, he continued.

"The weather was real bad. Even with a spotlight I couldn't see fifty feet in front of the boat."

"No compass, Jim?"

"I told you, Fred. Didn't have no compass. I just idling my way ahead, three, four miles an hour. I was a blind fella with sheets of water in my face, feeling my way. We was thrown around, water breakin over the bow and lightning all around us. Any second seem lightning would burn up the boat. I couldn't hold a course if I knew what course to hold. I was afraid we'd hit Piquet Rock or one of the Turtle Rocks. That would be the end of us. No one would ever find us in that wild ocean.

"Every time lightnin hit the water, I stare ahead and try to glimpse a rock. I pick my way from one rock to the next, like I was rock climbing stead of running a fishing boat. When I couldn't see, I prayin I didn't hit a breaking reef. I wait for a burst of light and then I see a rock and get my bearing for a minute or so. But through it, I figure I'd make it back. I'd show Banes and the guys. No one else would have tried it on such a night but I did."

"No white line, Jim?"

"Not on that night. Now fifty years later, it feel like a miracle making it through that fire and wild water. Feeling my way into Bimini harbor. But I made it, just like I told Banes and the others. Tied her up for the night. Man paid me four hundred. I went home and went to sleep."

"What about the sharks?" asked Doron.

"The story ain't quite finish," Jim answered.

"Around ten the following morning, on Cat Cay, Bradford Banes decide he want to get back to Bimini to see his family. He went to the captain of his boat, guy named Eddie Wall and say, 'Cap, let's go home.' Wall don't want to go cause the seas too rough. But Banes push him, and he argue if Jimmy could do it, they could make it easy. Their boat was a lot bigger than mine. Wall didn't want to go but was fed up with all of Banes's arguing and cursing.

"There was no more lightnin, but the wind was now blowing hard from the west, maybe thirty-five or forty knots. When it blow that way is a big surge comin cross the sand bar there in front of South Bimini. A boat has to get through big breakin seas to get in the harbor in such wind.

"When they get off Sunshine Inn, the boat was caught in the surge and fell onto her side. Brad sittin on the bridge on one of the chairs with his arms fold like he had no concern in the world. When the boat roll, Brad was toss right into the water. There was fellas working outside the Sunshine Inn, they see when he went over.

"Eddie Wall circle round and round for an hour, but he couldn't find Brad. They search the beach but they couldn't find him."

"They never found him?"

"Three days later, my mommy saw a body lyin on the beach or what was left of Banes after the sharks finish with him. She call some neighbors, and they pull him out. Then Ansel and I made a rough box. We knock it together in a few minutes. We wrap Banes in a sheet and put him in the box. Same time we was making the box, fellas was diggin the hole."

"He should have been holding on, Jim."

"No, Fred. Was his time. When it's time for a man to go, he'll go whether he's holdin on or not."

Jimmy nodded a couple of times before he stood up and slowly headed down to his bunk.

The three of us walked outside to take a last look before turning in. It was a beautiful night, clear, breezy, with a little chill in the air. Before going back in, I switched on the underwater lights, and the sharks were still patiently circling the boat, waiting.

In the morning the sharks were gone, but none of us was in the mood for a swim.

Part III

Even when Bobby was on top, he spent part of each day crafting sculpture from coral. In the heat of the afternoon, before he began preparing stocks and sauces for the French cuisine he would serve the boat owners, you'd see him standing outside a plywood shack down the road fifty yards from the clubhouse working with a noisy grinding tool. He was wearing a bandanna and goggles, his big Lab, Marlin, at his feet while he fashioned starfish, marlin, barracudas, turtles from grooved pieces of brain coral that he and Rasta dug up from the bottom of the lagoon. Bobby's face was matted in thick dust. He worked rapidly, with a steady hand, and though the work came together quickly, it was never glib or glitzy. Rather, Bobby's sculpture was primitive and heavy, as if excavated from the earth, which seemed unlikely given the speed with which he worked and coming from a man who seemed deeply invested in life's razzmatazz.

Many evenings, he was joined beside the shack by Rasta who watched like a hawk. Rasta wanted to learn how to make sculpture, and Bobby was teaching him. Then after a while, the two friends sat on a couple of crates that faced the tall rock cliffs that girdled the opposite side of the lagoon and protected the little harbor from storms. Bobby told Rasta his plans as he did many afternoons. He was going to build a five-star hotel in the rocks—blast and drill rooms into the cliffs in a style that had impressed him when he was on holiday in Matera, Italy, where rock cave houses were carved into the cliffs. It was a big unusual idea and Rasta took it in.

Then Bobby decided there wasn't enough stone for an entire hotel. Instead, they could fashion six or eight luxury apartments in the cliff, each of them with a balcony affording an incomparable view of the reef and the blue water beyond. Rasta imagined himself and Bobby blasting and drilling rooms into the rocks. *Why not?* They'd dredged the lagoon and made a harbor. They could do this.

Bobby predicted the luxury condos would lure back the wealthiest boat owners that had stopped visiting the island following the sad event with the Haitians. Bobby's biggest players had just felt uneasy about the whole episode, which ended with half-eaten corpses, their skin falling off, littering the beach within sight of the yachts and dining hall. Instead of Rum Cay, the high rollers now cruised their yachts to Turks and Caicos and the Virgin Islands. Really, it was understandable.

Bobby's plan to win them back entailed the new condos, building a dozen beachfront luxury homes, sprucing up the restaurant, and he and Rasta would need to add on an additional twelve hundred feet to the small landing strip in the center of the island so his patrons could bring in guests on their private jets. That would be easy enough.

Bobby estimated they'd clear ten million with his condo idea alone. Rasta would soon become a wealthy man.

Meanwhile, the marina was struggling. Most days in the slips there were only a half dozen boats owned by serious fishermen who raced down from Florida for several days of marlin and tuna action off the corner. These men operated much smaller boats burning only a small fraction of the fuel as the larger fishing yachts that had once frequented the island. Bobby's diesel sales were off nearly 80 percent. His new clientele didn't have thousands to burn on fancy dinners and wine in Bobby's restaurant. Instead, they grilled hamburgers on the dock and went to bed early. Most evenings there were only one or two couples eating Bobby's unrivaled cuisine, and sometimes he just kept the doors of the restaurant closed.

The millionaire yacht owners of the past had taken pleasure in tipping Bobby five or even ten thousand before casting off for the next island. In those days, Bobby had given a share of his tip money to Rasta who then had enough to live his modest life and to help out Biggy, who never had a dollar. And also, he gave money each month to Rosie, who was struggling to

keep her dilapidated pig farm operating. Bobby's new clientele didn't leave tips, or if they did, they might slip him fifty dollars.

~

In the late afternoon, Dennis drove his new jeep from his beach house to the marina and parked on the dirt road just north of Bobby's shed. With a nod he walked past Bobby and Rasta sitting on crates, making their plans.

Dennis smiled with squinting hooded eyes. He had plans of his own.

Bobby's dog, Marlin, tensed and growled at the hefty man with several days' growth of beard.

"It's OK, boy," said Bobby. Marlin didn't look so sure but settled again at Bobby's feet.

Dennis shuffled ahead, sniffing the air as if trying to pick up the scent of prey. He lived in the present, moving from one urge, one argument, one conquest to the next. He didn't value or even understand patience or compromise.

He turned the corner and slowly climbed up the path to the air-conditioned clubhouse, wiping sweat from his forehead with a thick hairy forearm.

He walked into the empty clubhouse and through the dining room where Flo's little girl played quietly with a small doll beneath one of the tables.

Dennis passed the child and stood in the kitchen doorway

while Flo leaned over the sink, washing the lunch dishes. Flo was humming an old Billie Holiday standard in her rich, deep voice.

Dennis closed his eyes and seemed to sway a little to her tune.

Flo heard something, turned around.

She registered his snickering smile and turned back to her work. She was no longer singing.

Most of all, Dennis trusted his needs and instincts. He always chose battlefields where he could win.

Dennis's body now ached with need.

He walked to Flo, turned her as if executing a crude dance routine. He reached for her large breast, then roughly pulled down her bra. She stood there accepting his rough handling. She knew it would be a big mistake to resist. Flo turned her head to the side when he put his hand under her light dress. Dennis pulled down her panties and then his underpants. She didn't say a word. She didn't make a sound. She never looked at him.

Dennis quickly ejaculated on the cement floor and gestured for Flo to clean it up. He pulled up his shorts and headed out the kitchen door and back through the dining room past the child and out the door into the heat of late afternoon.

He stood on the dining room porch for a minute or two looking at a roped-off area of Bobby's property that would soon become his hamburger bar. Dennis had made a deal with Bobby. For two hundred thousand, Bobby had agreed to make Dennis a 51 percent owner of a small hamburger bar with seating for about twenty people. Within the week, a barge from

Florida would come with supplies. Dennis had already flown in men from Miami who would soon begin constructing the facility on Bobby's property just south of the clubhouse.

Dennis shook his head. *Too small, much too small.* He walked down the hill to the markers slowly savoring the smell of Flo on his fingers. Dennis began moving the markers further down toward the marina's docks, greatly increasing the footprint of his bar.

~

Bobby didn't worry about the downturn in business. Since he was a kid fabricating his own skateboards and surfboards, he'd always made good money. Later on, when his custom car shop had gone belly up, he'd hired on as a freelancer for the DEA embedding himself in a Colombian drug operation working in the southern Bahamas. He was brash and gutsy and loved the life of a double. He made a half million in six months until he barely escaped with his life. For Bobby, making big money and spending it was breathing—inhale, exhale. In recent years, he'd kept a Ferrari in Miami, brought his lady of the month to clubs in South Beach, took groups of buddies to pricey restaurants, and always picked up the tab. Then he'd return to the island, sit beside the sculpting shed, and report his lifestyle and conquests to Rasta, who had never had any money to speak of.

Even during these difficult times, Bobby had nearly a

hundred thousand in the bank not including the check from Dennis who, for some reason, was anxious to throw even more money into the marina.

But now Bobby could barely think about the marina. He was crazy in love with a girl more than twenty years his junior and he would do anything to win her heart.

"She has me reaching," he said to Rasta. "She's just so fresh and alive."

Rasta nodded.

These days Bobby's huge friend walked with a limp from an arthritic hip and frequent flare-ups of gout. Some mornings it was too painful for Rasta to get out of bed.

"When she takes off her clothes, all the Bobby goes out of me. I can't say no to this girl."

For years, Bobby's women had been weary—that's how it seemed—or he'd grown weary with them. His seductions had become boozy and monotonous and forgettable, scores of women passing in a blur like his youth.

"She makes me shiver like an old horse . . . and she knows it, Rasta. The power she has. I'm always worried she's gonna leave me. I was always the one who did the leaving."

Rasta looked at the boats in the empty marina. He looked at the rock wall where they'd planned to build the grand hotel.

"Who is she?" he finally asked.

"Come on, man. You met her. She was studying art or some kind of writing in graduate school and I brought her here spring break. Don't you remember? Slim girl with long hair, always writing in a notebook."

Bobby looked at his old friend for affirmation that Hannah stood out for Rasta as well.

Rasta nodded to make his friend happy, but he didn't remember. Bobby had brought so many for a weekend.

Bobby would soon leave the island to take his bride-to-be to Europe for a three-month ultra-first-class vacation. He spoke of the resorts they'd visit, the wines they'd sample. Rasta nodded. "You'll be in charge here," Bobby said gesturing toward the docks that were empty but for an old charter boat from Key West and Mike's listing sailboat. When a shadow of doubt passed across Rasta's face, Bobby quickly added, "I'll take her to Matera in Italy and sketch the rock houses. When I get back, we'll get started blasting into the cliff." He gestured toward the rock wall across the lagoon.

～

Soon after Bobby left for Europe, Dennis directed his stateside building crew to put up a large guesthouse near his home several miles north on the beach road and right behind it, long trailer-shaped living quarters for a dozen of his workers who would remain on the island for future building projects. The dimensions of his property were now about four times the size of what he'd purchased from Bobby. After a month, he brought in more men from the States, and they went to work on his hamburger bar.

Dennis never considered Bobby's response to these unannounced or greatly expanded building projects. He trusted his instincts and moved ahead with his plans. Every two weeks, a barge from Miami came into the lagoon at high tide bringing appliances and building supplies. In the morning, Dennis looked over engineering drawings with his men and set them to work. Whenever he was in the mood, he visited Flo in the kitchen.

After three months, the finished hamburger bar was replete with icemakers that could service a three-hundred-seat restaurant, a large costly machine to desalinate water from the lagoon, and a custom twenty-foot grill to handle a hundred burgers at a time. The kidney-shaped facility now reached from Bobby's restaurant to the dock and nearly all the way to the cottages on the beach—an outsized architectural monstrosity that engulfed the petite marina that remained mostly empty. In late afternoon, after his lovemaking, Dennis walked out onto the back porch of Bobby's restaurant and admired his accomplishment.

~

Rasta's friend, Biggy, was a short, unassuming man, with a sad smile. For years, when the marina was in its prime, Biggy, showed up in late afternoon to watch the fancy boats work their way through the reef and enter the lagoon. With a mixture of expectation and melancholy, he watched swaggering captains power big boats into their slips while he stole glances at the young women in the stern. No one seemed to mind these evening visits by Biggy. Unlike some of the other locals who came to the marina, Biggy never pestered mates or captains for fish to take home. He mostly stood by in silence. Occasionally, one of the young women on the boats brushed against him with a smile as she passed on the narrow dock, or even lingered to say hello, standing so close he could smell her womanly aroma.

Once I asked him why he visited so faithfully, and Biggy surprised me with his candor. He came, he said, hoping to find a girl he could love. I didn't respond to this immediately. Honestly, I was too nonplussed and at the time I didn't fully understand his predicament. But during a subsequent conversation, I tried to suggest that perhaps the young girls visiting on the yachts might not offer the best chances for him. I wondered if Biggy might find a local girl in town or perhaps he might travel to Nassau with Rasta for a week where he might meet someone to love. Biggy listened attentively but didn't look convinced. Then he added, inexplicably, that girls are afraid of him. Still, Biggy remained hopeful that one afternoon his ship would come in.

Many evenings, and particularly with Bobby off the island, Biggy lingered in the marina for talks with Rasta. Usually the friends sat on weathered benches overlooking the lagoon. They enjoyed watching twelve-foot tiger and bull sharks gracefully cruise beneath the docks in their endless circling of the lagoon searching for food.

"Jealousy, yeah," said Rasta, answering his friend. "I feel Dennis just want the place. I don't know what he want it for. Not for the money. There's no money here. He want it for his own pleasure. He don't even like a bunch of people around him. He want it for hisself."

"Maybe he want to be Bobby?" offered Biggy.

Rasta mused a little. "You know, he just regretful of what Bobby have and the kind of relationship Bobby have with people," he said. "And the way Bobby live his life in the marina. That put a serious toll on Dennis . . . The way people look up to Bobby, admire him. Bobby don't have Dennis money, but he have something Dennis lack and that eat him. Maybe the marina give it to him."

Biggy was a wounded man, but also he was unduly wise and compassionate. Rasta watched out for him, tried to make him happy. One time he even paid a girl to give his friend an evening of pleasure, although that didn't work out so well.

It was Rasta who began calling his friend Biggy, and the name stuck. One afternoon the two friends had been conching on the flats in Bobby's Boston Whaler. Biggy was leaned way over the side looking for conch and crawfish on the bottom through a glass bottom bucket when Rasta glanced over at his friend. Rasta glimpsed a fat snake—a poisonous rock snake from the island, he presumed, that had climbed into the skiff and was working its

way from Biggy's knee up into his shorts. Rasta shouted and tried
to whack the creature away. That's when Biggy reached down
and curled his astonishing package back into his underwear.
Rasta was speechless. Had never seen anything like this before in
his life. His little friend possessed a thick donkey penis that hung
to his knee . . . A year or so earlier, when Rasta had paid a small
pretty young woman to make love to his friend, she'd run away
from Biggy. Now Rasta understood.

~

During the nearly four months Bobby traveled in Europe, the
marina became a virtual ghost town. Besides Dennis's workers, there were no visitors. A pack of hungry dogs had moved
from the tiny village and had settled on Bobby's property.
Mostly in the heat of day, they slept under trees or in the shade
of buildings, but in the evening they raced around, barking,
chasing dock cats, and foraging for food.

The boats from Florida stopped coming altogether. The big
game fishing community is quite small, and fishermen in the States
knew that Bobby was away. Most of them traveled to the island
to feast and drink with Bobby, to feel his life force and implicit
promise of a long wild ride ahead—even for the oldies—with infi-
nite land deals and fiery sunsets falling into the blue water.

Rasta was left in charge of nothing. He had no money. He
was shepherding the empty place for his friend. Once or twice

a week, a transient boat pulled into the dock to buy a little fuel. Occasionally one of these boat owners paid Rasta with cash. He put the money in his pocket—perhaps it came to a thousand dollars a month. He felt shitty stealing from his friend but he needed money to buy food and pay his electric bill. He waited for Bobby to begin constructing condos in the cliff, for the party nights to ramp up again with naked fire dancing on the beach and the morning's deafening roar of mega fishing yachts racing up to the corner for marlin action.

~

After nearly four months, Bobby flew back to Rum Cay. He buzzed the island astonished to see his marina swallowed whole by Dennis's hamburger bar. He saw the new buildings leeching from Dennis's property on the north end of the beach and two new guesthouses near the marina beside his three more modest ones. He saw a barge laden with supplies nearing the entrance to the lagoon.

By the time Bobby got to his marina, the barge was about to tie onto his dock. It was loaded with large refrigerators and freezers for the hamburger bar, two diesel generators to run the operation whenever the aged generator on the island shut down, sundry supplies, and stacks of wood and electrical hookups for future projects Dennis was planning.

Bobby ordered the barge captain to get off his dock.

"I thought this was Dennis's dock," the captain answered.

"Dennis's dock? Since when? Get that shit out of here."

The two men argued for a few more minutes until the island's only police officer drove up. When Bobby refused to back off, the officer rested a hand on his pistol grip and told Bobby he was going to take him in.

"Take me in for what? This is my fucking place!"

Bobby was led to the police car and driven to the one-room jail in town where he was locked up.

~

"Why Bobby let Dennis in here?" asked Biggy later that night while the two friends sat on the old dock bench slapping mosquitoes.

"Bobby, he figure out the money Dennis have," Rasta answered ruefully. "That's the big thing for Bobby. He always lookin for easy money . . . He figure he can handle Dennis . . . But Bobby movin too fast to see . . . Bobby go away four months and Dennis do favors for guys. He ask police sergeant, you need money to send your wife off island, no problem; you need a vehicle or a new engine for the skiff? Dennis take care of it. Fellas think Dennis a generous man. But come a time he call on you, you do what he say . . . you better do what he say cause Dennis own you . . . Dennis an aggressive person and he obsess with the marina. He can't think about nothin else. He'll lose his own family to get what he want . . . When he want something, he'll die to get it done."

Part IV

It occurs to me, I've become another old fella sitting in a chair reflecting on the glory years. I enjoy replaying trolling days with my dad on his forty-foot fishing boat and years later, pulling baits and lures with my wife and kids on boats I've owned. I can still feel the sting of big fish that got away—how it seemed life changing to lose that bluefish or striped bass or tuna right beside the boat—except I'm not doing my elegiac reflecting on a bench in the park. I'm sitting in a creaky swivel chair on the weathered bridge of my forty-year-old boat steering south from Conception Island into rough, remote waters.

Jimmy is sitting with me on the bridge, lost in thought. He's put on weight in the past year and now walks with a limp. If we hook a marlin in this choppy sea, he'll have trouble making it down the ladder into the cockpit to help out. While I focus on the lures behind us, Jim looks ahead of the boat so we don't smack into another vessel, though we haven't seen another boat in two days. Jim doesn't want to talk about whatever's wrong, which is OK with me. I don't want to talk either.

But that's not exactly true. I want Jim the way I knew him. I'm annoyed by this new reticence and dour expression. I try to stare at the lures.

John and Doron are down below resting or chatting or eating—I don't know what they're doing. Although most likely, John is making a drawing of Doron. He's usually drawing one of us. Even in heavy seas, with the boat slamming and pitching, he works on his drawings with a steady hand. John always goes for something he feels inside his subject—some festering secret that informs the picture. That's more important to him than an exact physical likeness. I always want to steal a look. I wonder what he'll find in Doron, who keeps painful stories locked deep inside.

Yesterday, John was drawing me on the bridge. We were about an hour out from Columbus Point when he suddenly bolted from his chair, hustled down the ladder, and started puking over the side. He couldn't stop vomiting. John had never been to sea before this trip. What was I going to do with him out here? But after twenty minutes, he'd washed his face and he was back on the bridge working on his picture of me at the helm.

Eventually, I stop thinking about this and that and concentrate on my four lures following the boat. Three of them are skipping and diving like lovely little tunas. But one of the lures has sucked down beneath the surface. I try to will it back up on top to join the others. No luck. I try to focus my attention on the three lures that are properly rolling up and down the white-water wake, but the one stuck below is annoying the hell out of me.

I call down to Doron. "Hey, Doron!" He doesn't hear me. I call again. Finally I stomp on the deck of the bridge until he looks up. I tell Doron to pull in the lure and take a look at it. He winds the lure to the boat at record speed. He's so excited to catch fish. The lure has a braid of seaweed trailing from the hook. He clears the lure and puts it back out. Doron looks up at me and I nod, to say, *Yeah, it's riding better now.* When he sees that I look satisfied, Doron looks satisfied. I am the lord of answers out here.

In recent years, I've fallen in love with watching the lures. Soon after putting them in the water, I stop daydreaming about old fishing adventures or problems back in the city. I love the dance of baits and lures across the surface. I can watch them for hours on end without feeling bored.

I enjoy this trance state so much that when a small tuna or mahi-mahi comes up behind one of the lures, and gets hooked, it feels like a bother. I quickly want to get my lure back out and following the boat. It is hard to explain this manifestation of eccentricity, even to myself. One of the embarrassing secrets of my fishing life is that I sometimes steer away from schools of fish lest the imposition of hooked fish will disturb the tranquility of the search and troll.

Meanwhile, these two friends of mine, Doron and John Mitchell are on fire with wanting to catch a big blue marlin. They don't know how. Doron knows a little—he's caught a small one—but neither of them truly understands the strength and speed of these great animals, the dangers involved with catching one. They are counting on me to find one and show them how to do it.

I was steering for the north end of Long Island, a desolate patch of ocean where I'd caught large yellowfin tuna in the past. For hours the wind had been falling off. The ocean looked gray and cold as if we were fishing up north on a cloudy day. Then the weather turned weird, very weird. The wind came quickly and the seas turned white and sharp. A shower of water on the bridge jolted me from reveries.

In several minutes, waves built to four feet, then six- and eight-footers were bunched tight together. In minutes, we were in a full-on gale though there were no storm clouds in any direction. Why all this wind? What were we headed into? Green water began spilling across the bow. I needed to push the throttles ahead, so I wouldn't bury the bow. But with the increased speed, we were slamming into head seas and the anchor on the bow was smacking down onto the pulpit. Damn it. I'd forgotten to check that the anchor was properly secured. It was too rough to send anyone up there to do it now.

Doron looked up at me from below with a concerned expression, *We OK, Cap?* I nodded, no sweat, though I was sweating. My boat was falling off waves and skittering sideways. I was wrestling with the wheel to keep her bow into it, so she wouldn't broach. I'd been sitting at my desk in the city for the last seven months working on a screenplay about two mismatched lovers. Suddenly I was a captain in a big sea in the middle of nowhere with a crew of greenhorns.

She's a tough old boat. Made it through a lot of bad weather and always got us home. But I was hoping we didn't get a big strike out here. I thought about pulling in the lines. It would be impossible to handle a big fish in this rolling white mess—not with this crew. But also, I wanted my guys seated and holding on—I didn't want a painter or cabinetmaker lost over the side. It was too rough to bring in the lures. So the lures stayed out there, jumping from wave to wave.

After about an hour, the mystery wind slackened a little, still rough but waves weren't so close together, manageable conditions. The *Ebb Tide* became easier to steer. I relaxed a little.

About the same time I spotted the rocky windward side of Long Island I heard line click off one of the reels. Unless I imagined it. Then I heard it again, but I couldn't see anything in the white water.

Then I saw it, glimpsed it . . . *Really? Really?*

When a big marlin rises from the sea to snatch a lure, it is so odd and majestic and fast as a scream of iridescent colors in the air, one is tempted to call it a fantasy. When such moments happen, with a skeleton, inexperienced crew, there is a lot of confusion about what's taking place. People look at one another frozen in place.

And I'm screaming, "MARLIN, MARLIN!"

But in our boat, there was no one in the cockpit. Line was now spilling off the reel while I called for Doron and John. Where were they? Probably down below, making a drawing.

"Come on, John." I began stomping on the deck. "COME ON, JOHN. WHAT THE FUCK!"

The marlin swam across our wake, and I could see the full heft of it. More than four hundred pounds, maybe five hundred.

Then the line seemed to go slack. Shit. It broke off. No one even saw the damn fish but me.

But no, no, there it was again, all twelve feet of it jumping behind the boat. Shaking its head, my lure in its beaked mouth.

The marlin was now sprinting right at the boat, the bill aimed dead center of the transom. I slammed the throttles ahead trying to get away from the fish—so it wouldn't jump into the cockpit.

"Where's John?" I screamed, pounding on the deck with my shoe.

The marlin barely missed the boat, shot ahead of us. I spun the boat around so the stern was again facing the fish. Began to back down.

Finally John poked his head out from down below.

"Where you been?"

"Making lunch . . . Now it's all over the floor. A whole jar of raspberry jelly all over the floor."

"Look behind the boat. A blue marlin—look at it jump!"

The hooked marlin was jumping two hundred yards astern of us.

John looked, but he didn't know what he was looking for or where. John was looking high in the sky as if searching for rare birds.

Finally, with Doron's help, John climbed into the fighting chair and started cranking the big reel with his considerable strength.

John is a marathon runner. He's lean, wiry, and powerful—but he didn't know the first thing about angling. The marlin was sprinting away from us, line spinning off the reel, and John was cranking away.

"Don't reel, John," I called down into the wind. "The fish is running."

"What," he called back. "What?"

"Stop reeling," I yelled trying to be heard above the wind and diesels. "When the fish stops running, then pull the rod up with your left arm and reel in slack on the down swing."

John turned around and screamed back, "What, what Fred?" Then he went back to cranking the big reel as though life depended on it.

"Stop reeling!" I screamed.

"What? What?" John kept cranking harder, faster.

Each time I called down a direction, John or Doron screamed back, "What Fred? Speak up!" I guess I have a small voice. My beginner crew was operating in the blind with only fragmentary wind tossed advice from Fred.

After five or seven minutes of this fruitless winding, John's arm froze like a plank of wood. He couldn't wind anymore. By now the fish had stopped running, was ready to come to the boat, but John was breathing heavily and couldn't move his arm. He turned back and looked up at me with a helpless expression.

"Wind, John. Wind, wind, wind."

"I can't, Fred," he said, looking stricken.

I considered climbing off the bridge to help. But if I came down from the controls and the fish sprinted at the boat, we could have a tragedy.

Doron coaxed John to wind the reel with his other arm. John now began cranking with two hands on the reel, and the fish was getting close. The marlin jumped a couple of times right behind the boat glowing a brilliant blue and silver. Doron so excited, as if witnessing a birth.

Then I noticed Jim climbing down the ladder. I called to him to get back up here. What if he fell in that heaving sea and broke a leg. Who would run the grocery store? Who would lift cases of Coke and beer for his old wife?

But Jim didn't listen and was soon standing against the

transom with his big hand poised to grab the heavy mono-filament leader.

I was slowly backing the boat toward the fish, Jim reaching out to grab the leader, and in that moment, he stopped being my creaky, overweight, elderly friend Jim. He was spry and strong, the powerhouse Jimmy he'd been fifty years earlier when he'd had a reputation as the best big game wire man in the Bahamas.

Jim grabbed the leader, with one hand, then the next and after three sweeping pulls toward him, the twelve-foot fish was swimming alongside the boat. John got out of the chair, stood beside Jim, and looked at his fish. Then he turned back to me, his face all red and sweaty from effort and thrill.

Jim snatched out the hook and we all watched the tired marlin head back down into the deep blue.

Around dusk we anchored on the leeward side of a small atoll off the north end of Long Island. I was hoping for a calm night on the hook, but around midnight dishes fell out of the cabinets and the timbers of the old boat began to creak. The southeast wind had clocked around to the west, and the boat was rolling badly in the surge. We all had to hold on to stay in our bunks and no one slept very much.

One more day at sea and we'd arrive at Rum Cay.

Part V

After two nights in the small rotting town jail, Bobby was released with a stern warning to leave Dennis alone.

"Or you'll be right back in here, or worse," the police sergeant warned.

"What do you mean, worse?"

Bobby slowly ambled back a half mile along the dirt road to the marina, trying to make sense of what had happened to his life. He walked past the little shack where he'd made sculpture most evenings, but that ardent work now seemed remote and unappealing. Bobby was distracted by thoughts of his young bride and their great passion. It was hard to pull himself back. He didn't feel like the man who had dived into feeding sharks to save drowning Haitian youngsters.

Dennis was standing beside his pickup truck speaking to one of his men. He looked up at Bobby, smiled with squinting pig eyes. He looked back at his plans for a fourth new guest-house on the beach.

It occurred to Bobby one of them was lost in a dream.

"Hey, man, come on," he said to Dennis, reaching for the past, when Dennis had followed him around the marina like a puppy.

Standing on the path just below his empty dining room, Bobby felt a surge of the old Bobby. He knew how to make promises. He knew how to charm. He could handle Dennis.

Dennis's building manager walked over, asked a question.

Bobby grinned at Dennis as he had in the dining room crammed with high rollers. Dennis had reached for Bobby then, tried to gain his eye. Dennis had had to wait his turn. Bobby was probing for the right way to work his way back inside.

Bobby smacked Dennis on the shoulder. "We never discussed any of this. You can't build a city in my marina."

Bobby started to laugh. It was funny. It really was funny. Like a clichéd old Western when the rich bad guy comes into town, makes threats, and drives honest settlers away, takes over all the land. Dennis laughed as well—two buddies sharing a joke.

"Really, man? What were you thinking?"

"I don't think so much," Dennis answered without irritation or surprise. It was true. He didn't think too much. Dennis heeded needs and instincts above all else. And Bobby's return to the island had freed him in a way he couldn't yet define. Dennis felt bolstered, energized.

"You can't do this, man."

Dennis nodded once, walked a few paces to his pickup, reached inside, and showed Bobby a stack of building permits with official seals from the Ministry of Works and Utilities in Nassau. Everything looked in order.

"You see?" Dennis said, putting the papers away. And he shrugged, to say, *Yes, I can. What will you do about it?*

~

Meanwhile, in the ruined sailboat, Mike wrote feverishly on his laptop. Locals coming by the marina saw less and less of him, and by the time Dennis erected his hamburger bar, Mike had virtually disappeared. It's a mystery how he lived, where he got food and fresh drinking water, how he washed himself, how he survived the onslaught of mosquitoes and sand fleas after a rain. He might have died and rotted below, although on sleepless nights Biggy occasionally walked down to the marina, and he told Rasta that a couple of times he spotted a skinny white man pacing the docks at two in the morning.

For years Mike listened to traces of the world carried on the wind and fashioned them into a vision he was continually revising. He worked away in the hot cramped boat as if looking up at the island, the marina, and lagoon from beneath the earth, reporting on a limbo world inhabited by dreamlike characters. He revised endlessly, became fed up and began again. But when Bobby returned to the transformed marina, Mike felt empowered with new confidence. He listened to Bobby talking with Dennis, almost begging and he was stunned and delighted. This new Bobby, needy, a little pathetic, was much more appealing to Mike. He wanted to capture every twitch of Bobby's shedding skin as if he'd been waiting all this time to witness it. What would happen to this new Bobby? As Dennis built his fancy cottages and did finishing work on his massive hamburger bar, Mike's fictive marina grew more and more shadowy and diaphanous. The high rollers and their trophy girls were still there but they were ghostly now—one could walk right through them. In a later draft, sharks and tarpon swam through folks on the dock as if the ghost marina was now inhabiting the bottom of the lagoon. Mike began to love Bobby whom he had previously loathed. Finally, in Mike's later chapters, the marina disappeared entirely—the whole thing was swept away by some apocalypse he didn't yet understand. Where did it go? What happened to Bobby? He tried to figure this out as he refined his pages. He knew the ending must relate to the doomed Haitian boat and the lingering ghosts of drowning children. Through his porthole, Mike watched them at night chanting, dancing, shaking rattles on the ruined dock, their skin falling off in sheets while the boat owners and their naked girls looked on in disgust. And what about the final chapter? Could he fashion a surprise, a happy ending without seeming banal? Mike struggled with his novel that grew and grew as he withered to little more than bones. His book was fifteen hundred pages long when Mike suffered his own tragedy—but that came later.

~

Bobby and Rasta walked up the steep winding path to the old stone house Bobby's parents built thirty years earlier. Bobby needed to sort things out but couldn't bring himself to think about Dennis.

"He's an idiot," he said to Rasta, who nodded. He wanted to swat Dennis like an insect.

The house was worn down, raunchy and beautiful from the battering of storms and the filth of Bobby's animals. The place had held together through a dozen hurricanes.

The friends stood together on the bluff across from the marina looking out to sea. To the southeast, Bobby squinted into the afternoon sun and counted five or six boats trolling off the corner of the island. They were far away, hardly more than smudges on the horizon.

"Hey, man," Bobby offered Rasta a high five. "We're back."

The captains of these boats were surely friends of his that had heard he was returning to Rum Cay.

There was so much riding on a glimpse. But of course the entire island was hardly more than a smudge or a glimpse— one wave could totally wash away Rum Cay with so much hope and tragedy resting a few feet above sea level.

"In two weeks there'll be twelve trolling out there," he said to Rasta.

There were things Rasta wanted to say, more tangible and immediate than the good times Bobby presumed. There was only one policeman on the island, and Dennis now owned him. There were other men who would do his bidding whenever he asked, whatever he asked. Bobby didn't get it. Bobby was still in France with the girl.

"I need to clean this place up," Bobby said with a guilty smile. "Hannah's arriving in a week."

Bobby shared the house with five big Labs, including Marlin who had sired the others. There were also a few goats that wandered in and out of Bobby's several rooms filthy with animal hair and the smell of goat urine. Bobby cherished his dogs but especially Marlin who slept in Bobby's bed.

"Maybe you and Flo would help me for couple days?"

Rasta nodded OK. But his mind had gone to the night he and Biggy had been fishing for snappers on the dock when several of Dennis's workers captured a few of the town dogs that had been hanging around the outdoor bar barking and whimpering for food. The men petted the animals, fed them scraps of hamburger while tying them together with a dock line. Then, as Dennis directed, the men dragged the heaving package of animals onto the dock and kicked them over. Within a minute, bull sharks torpedoed the frantic drowning dogs. The men laughed while the sharks tore the dogs apart.

Biggy had gestured to the pitch-black water when it had grown quiet. "Maybe Dennis, he pay . . . he pay a fella a few bucks to slit Bobby and toss him to the sharks . . . Never worry a day about it."

"Bobby a hunter, you know," answered Rasta. "A serious hunter. Bobby can kill you with an arrow from a long way."

Bobby and Rasta stood in the yard littered with dog shit and loose clumps of goat feces. Rasta knew if his friend felt threatened, he'd walk down the hill and punch Dennis in the face.

Bobby grabbed his billy goat by the horns. The beast smelled like a latrine that hadn't been cleaned in a month. He began wrestling with the goat until they were both filthy rolling on the ground and Bobby was beaming.

Rasta didn't say anything about Dennis. He didn't mention that a few days before Bobby came back Dennis offered him sixty thousand dollars to cross over and Rasta said, "Shove it up your ass." That's when it first dawned on Rasta that he'd have to leave the island. Rasta walked back to his one room across the yard and crawled into bed. He didn't come down to the marina for three days.

~

Bobby's willowy young wife came off the small plane from Nassau holding a fancy writing pad. She couldn't contain herself, noting impressions of her first hours on the island. She was intoxicated by the soft evening breeze and Bobby's boyish delight to put it all into her hand—all he'd made and was going to make still. He'd shoveled and chiseled this place from sand and stone. Bobby could build houses and fix any machine that broke. He cooked meals like their favorite chefs in Lyon. Bobby crafted bold sculptures and placed them all around the marina, markers that illuminated the magic world he'd created. She wrote paragraphs about him in her notebook. Hannah had an idea for a little book of poetry that could be illustrated by lovely drawings of the island.

Hannah called her husband an artist. He wondered about what that meant and if it were true. She talked about opening a little store down by the gas dock where he could sell his sculptures. And maybe, she mentioned this tremulously while barely shaking her head no, maybe someday they could sell her book of verse. While she offered this, a sadness settled onto her face that he'd never noticed before. Bobby said, "Sure."

Boaters began to come back to the island, not the big yachts but the smaller boats from Miami and Lauderdale and the Florida Keys. Bobby was making some money pumping diesel and collecting dockage. Some nights there were twenty-five or thirty guys drinking and eating burgers at Dennis's place.

For several weeks Bobby worked on his docks, put in new pilings with Rasta's help, pumped fuel, went home late, played with his dogs, made love to his wife.

What a life! Hannah yelped each time one of Bobby's five dogs chased a rat through the kitchen. The dogs were bigger than Hannah, and when she walked into the house one or another of them jumped up and knocked her off balance. Stinking animals and water bugs the size of her hand walking the walls. After two weeks of heavy rain, mosquitoes and sand fleas were attacking in swarms. Hannah's arms and legs became red and swollen from innumerable bites. Bobby said she shouldn't worry, in time her body would become used to the bites. It was part of the life here. *Great.* She always smelled of dog, and there was no hot water in the shower. No neighborhood bookstore where she could peruse the poetry section. No one around to talk to. But she was game.

The youngest of the Labs, Cisco, was the first to win her heart. Whenever she felt lonely, Cisco came over and put his face into her hand. He seemed to feel her moods. Cisco looked pleased when she began taking notes and uneasy when she fretted. She fancied Cisco was encouraging her to write. Next she discovered Marlin, the oldest. He was a sage. He watched over the brood, growled when the young dogs stepped out of line. Hannah tried to read his mind. In the afternoons, she talked to Marlin about her new life here.

At night Bobby came home, shyly kissed her on the cheek, stalling, no, he wasn't hungry, maybe later, chitchat about the marina, how are the dogs doing, coaxing, fretting, without a word about it, until she turned to him, casually took off her shirt. She found his urgency so curious, so different than boys she'd known in school. Bobby was intoxicated by the sight of her body, wanted to kiss under her arms, inhale her. It was such a big deal to him. Like he was breathing her youth.

Hannah wrote notes about the heat, the bugs, her fears and curiosity, her unexpected vulnerability, and a glimmer of darkness inside. *Where would that lead?* She was a Brooklyn girl, a wannabe poet living alone with large animals, her new family, because Bobby was rarely around during the day. Hannah was entering the outskirts of the heart of darkness. She laughed at herself. But she'd long believed that great writing depended upon the exploration of darkness.

She plunged into it, started drinking wine in the afternoon while she waited for Bobby to come home, took notes, fed the dogs, washed them so they didn't smell so horribly. She was dissatisfied by her sentences, hoped the great ones would come later. Mysteries would pour out of her, unexpectedly. But the mystery was his passion for her when she took off her clothes. Hannah had wanted to write *Othello*. Instead, she herself was the work of art Bobby adored. She

FRED WAITZKIN

tried to relish it, to make him happy. Bobby, who had made
this whole island world.

~

Dennis had put a lot of money into the marina. He'd built
fancy cottages and the biggest outdoor bar in the Bahamas.
He'd installed a new water maker big enough to supply most
of the island with fresh water. He paid off clerks and judges
in Nassau, and they gave him a folder of officially stamped
documents. In his mind, the marina was now his. He could do
whatever he wanted.

What do you want, Dennis?

Dennis enjoyed the sensation of waiting. As if he were
watching himself grow larger and more powerful. He watched
the boats pull into the slips, his slips. Dennis visited Flo in
the kitchen whenever he felt a craving. He never noticed her
loathing. He barely noticed her at all.

Bobby and Dennis walked around one another. For a few
months, everything hung in the balance.

More boats visited the island. Some evenings every slip in
the marina was filled.

For ten years Rasta had operated the small bar inside Bobby's restaurant. The profit from this business was his to keep.
He also owned three beat-up ATVs that Bobby rented out to
guests to explore the island, gave the fees to Rasta. That had

82

all dried up, but now with the boats coming back, Rasta began stocking the shelves in the bar.

The fishing was exceptional that season. Often in the afternoons boats came into the marina flying one or two or sometimes three small flags on an outrigger to announce they'd caught marlin. Locals came down to the docks for a slab of yellowfin tuna or a barracuda.

Flo continued to do chores for Bobby, but she no longer brought her pudgy little girl with her to work. Flo cleaned Bobby and Hannah's breakfast dishes in the clubhouse kitchen, tidied the cottages on the beach, and then before leaving she took down the wash from the line. But she no longer sang her lushly phrased versions of "God Bless the Child" and "Summertime." Flo no longer sang at all. From time to time, one of the regulars asked about her singing and Flo looked confused, as though she had been mistaken for another woman from town. When she finished her work, Flo walked thirty minutes along the dirt road to the outskirts of Port Nelson to retrieve her daughter from her mother's farm, which was just north of the cemetery.

Part VI

I made a mistake. About noon on the last day of our troll to Rum Cay, we spotted several frigatebirds circling close to the water. I eased the *Ebb Tide* beneath the large swooping birds, quickly hooked one big mahi-mahi, about thirty pounds. She came aboard thrashing and glowing iridescent yellow, blue, and green. It seemed tragic to kill such a beauty, but after a brief discussion we put the fish in a cooler for our dinner that first night in Bobby's marina.

Near the coast, mahi-mahi are often wary of boats, but out here in the middle of the ocean, they were curious and remained close to the *Ebb Tide*. Doron and John wanted to cast to them with spinning tackle. After catching one and letting it go, John put down his rod, grabbed a drawing pad, and stood beside Doron, tried to capture a likeness of these beauties jumping, twisting, sprinting just below the surface. But the fish were too fast and John looked frustrated. He wanted to keep trying, but we still had a long way to go. It was more than an hour before I put the *Ebb Tide* back on course. I realized we'd be late getting in.

By the time I spotted the bluffs marking the north side of Rum Cay, it was after six. It took us another hour and a half to reach the barrier reef that ran along the south side of the island. It was seven thirty, and Rum Cay was shrouded in darkness.

I'd messed up . . . badly. I'd expected to see red markers beside the reefs leading into Bobby's harbor, but there weren't any buoys I could make out. Looking east I couldn't see any entrance into the harbor. I could barely see thirty feet in front of the boat, no moonlight.

Everyone looked at me for what to do. "Can you see the white line?" I asked Jimmy. He didn't even smile. What was the best of difficult alternatives? I wasn't sure. I might have idled around for twelve hours offshore of the reef. But I didn't want to handle the boat in the ocean until dawn. I was exhausted and wanted a beer and dinner.

I headed the *Ebb Tide* toward the middle of the bay. If we could work our way around a few coral heads, we might be able to drop anchor close to shore.

Doron went to the bow of the *Ebb Tide*, climbed out on the pulpit. He peered into the darkening water like a Viking, alive with the responsibility of guiding us in. He had the best eyes on the boat. He pointed to each coral head and yelled up to the bridge, "Turn starboard. Now straight ahead for fifty feet . . . hard to the left, more to the left!"

Honestly, I felt unhinged. I was steering blind, couldn't see a thing but glare on the shallow water. One mistake and we were wrecked. The overhead light on my bridge seemed to be broken and I could barely see my controls, kept reminding myself where the throttles were. I looked thoughtfully at the GPS though I didn't trust the accuracy of my readings so close to the shore in this reef littered bay. If we hit and broke the props and shafts, how would I ever get her back to Florida? Doron was our white line. He kept pointing the way. "To the starboard . . . hard to the port . . . straight ahead." I was only guessing, but Doron seemed to know. I steered where he said, and we edged our way in.

When I gauged that we were a hundred yards off the beach, I signaled to Doron to drop the hook. I knew we'd swing with the current and wind—maybe we'd plow into a coral head in the night, but there was nothing to do about it—nothing I could think of.

Our mahi-mahi was delicious, but my uneasiness persisted. I felt like I was waking from a dream I've had where I'm at a party but I've lost my pants. I walk among the guests in my underwear asking people if they will loan me pants to wear. People are surprised by my appearance, but no one will give me pants.

After dinner John began making a drawing of me in his large black book of secrets. I tried to pretend I was fully dressed. What kind of captain loses his pants, loses his bearings? I wondered if he would draw me without my pants.

The boat was quiet enough on the hook, but still I didn't sleep very well. I kept worrying about what happened to the red markers leading into the marina. If they were all gone, how would we find our way in in the morning? After three years, could I find my way through the jungle of reefs? And if I could, what would we find there?

We went to sleep with a lot of unresolved questions—channel markers were the least of it. More than we knew had happened on Rum Cay in the past three years.

Part VII

Most of the visiting boat crews had been having evening drinks and burgers at Dennis's bar. Dennis held court with a contemptuous smile, avoiding eye contact as though it were contagion. The atmosphere in his place was rowdy and festive with a hint of malice. Around ten each night, before the fishermen turned in, Dennis had one of his men bring buckets of tuna and wahoo guts to the water's edge. Then with spotlights blazing, the men tossed the entrails in the water and everyone watched the bull sharks attack like gigantic piranhas. Dennis relished the spectacle.

It was Bobby who altered the balance. For weeks he'd steered clear of his presumptive partner, pumped fuel, repaired, and puttered around the marina. But it galled him that Dennis's business was succeeding and that his former customers were laughing with Dennis, toasting sunsets with him.

Bobby decided to begin hosting potluck dinners in his dining room. In the old days, when the marina had been visited by super yachts, Bobby had held potlucks each Sunday night. All the boaters would contribute something delicious while Bobby concocted his storied dishes in the kitchen. In this new incarnation, Bobby provided all the food and did the cooking himself. One night he served the fishermen tuna tartare and coq au vin, the next night, cassoulet or boeuf bourguignon, each night another masterpiece.

Bobby didn't charge a penny for these meals. He'd set out to break Dennis's back with French cuisine served with largesse and charm. Why would anyone choose hamburgers?

Between manning the dock and dinners, Bobby was working eighteen-hour days. There wasn't time for Hannah's investigations and darkening moods.

All hands on deck.

"We'll close him down," he said to his wife before asking her to help run the bar business with Rasta.

Bobby was on fire with his food war and seemed to be winning.

Hannah tried to brighten herself for Bobby, dressed sexy in a short skirt and top showing a lean, tanned midriff. She was gorgeous, and no one noticed or cared about her melancholy. Even at half speed, she was smart and quick. Rasta was slow, had trouble keeping up with the rush of orders, made mistakes, particularly now when he had one foot out the door, his mind on the next life.

Hannah covered for him, happily. She found Rasta curious, inexplicable, and deep as the blue water. At the end of the night she'd ask him questions about his loneliness, or his enigmatic religion, and she became infatuated by the cadence of his sentences, his music, the way his odd language constructions wormed deep into the ecstasy or pain of a moment. Other times his voice rolled in like the surf. She stood at the bar listening to him speak to customers, or placing orders on the phone for supplies. She fancied him Othello. She wanted to put his voice into her poems, make it her own. She admired Rasta but also his mystery and wisdom made her feel like a poseur. Hannah wanted to be deep and enduring like the poets she studied in school, but she feared she had little to say. Rasta was all of these things and he didn't write anything at all. *Maybe that was a clue.* Hannah wanted to crawl into his skin. She whispered painful secrets to him she could barely say to herself. He nodded, surrounded her in his huge arms. He might have taken her anywhere.

When Bobby decided Rasta should share the bar profits with Hannah, she felt humiliated and tried to talk him out of it. But Rasta only shrugged. Empty promises had become the language of this place.

After two days of potluck dinners, fishermen stopped going to the mammoth outdoor bar. Bobby met the boats at the dock and invited them to the clubhouse for dinner. Bring your whole crew. Bobby's rekindled joie de vivre spiced his culinary masterpieces. Most nights, there weren't more than three or four guys sitting on Dennis's costly benches looking at their feet.

Bobby was winning. He stayed in the club a couple of hours after Hannah left, cleaning up, shaking hands, holding court about the future with a few night owls.

When he arrived back at the house on the hill, it was usually past midnight and he piled into bed, inviting Marlin to join him and Hannah. She found him greatly distracted, couldn't listen to a word she said. He was totally focused on the marina war.

Bobby could sense Dennis. He knew the storm was coming, but from what direction? He'd survived many storms.

~

There was the morning he told her Rasta was considering leaving the island, going back to Nassau to live in the big house with his family. Bobby insisted they didn't need him anymore. She could run the bar. They'd be fine.

Hannah was jolted. Anything but fine. Rasta gave color and depth to the lonely sand-swept place. How long could she remain on the island acting the role of Bobby's virgin bride?

Hannah needed to talk to Bobby, there were things he didn't know about her, but he insisted he had to get down to the dock. He was trying to starve Dennis out. He laughed. "I'll drive him away with food."

Bobby was loved by the fishermen who cruised 400 miles to troll the corner and dine at Sumner Point. He tried to explain this to her while he quickly got dressed. He pulled on his shorts, mentioned that Rasta had stolen from him when they were in Europe, pocketed the fuel money. "I have to let him go."

She put her hands to her ears, shook her head, *No, no, no.*

"Got to go. We'll talk later."

Hannah rushed out of the room wearing her red slip. She came back in a minute holding something in her hand. She was shaking like a leaf.

"I was a child myself," she managed. "I was crazy. I'm crazy now. Why does he have to go, Bobby? You love him."

Bobby tied his laces, looking past her. Who would pump the fuel?

Don't tell him now, Hannah. Later on. Some other day.

Her face was twisted horribly. It was bursting out of her like the baby girl she was guarding so closely. Her one true thing.

Hannah held the picture of a baby in her hand.

But the boats were waiting to head offshore. Who would pump the fuel?

"She was so perfect. She loved me. No one ever loved me like that tiny girl."

"What are you telling me? Why are you telling me this now?"

"I was a baby myself. I didn't know what to do with her." Hannah's chest was caved in with grief like an arthritic old woman.

Bobby shivered at the sight. The boats were waiting at the fuel dock.

Later that night, when he came home, she was sitting at the wooden table in her red slip from the morning, drinking wine. There were four small pictures of her baby daughter laid out in front of her. Bobby had had no idea his young wife had been a mother, had nursed a baby with her adolescent breasts. He couldn't put his arms around this news. He couldn't have been more surprised to learn she'd once been a terrorist. Bobby wasn't sure if he was devastated by the news or offered a brand-new chance.

Bobby coaxed her into the bedroom. He talked to her quietly about the marina. She shook her head, *No. Not interested.* He pulled off her slip, but she covered her breasts with her hands. *Why, Hannah? Why?* After a while, he made love to her, and her face gathered into such a deep sadness it seemed to embrace all of the tragedies on this island before and what was yet to come. Hannah cried while he held her, her sadness deepened further and was something he couldn't touch with all of his charm and optimism. It was beyond him. That's when he truly began to love her.

Part VIII

Two weeks later.

Rasta decided not to take his things back to Nassau—he wanted to start fresh. The day before he left the island, he hitched his trailer onto his battered jeep without a reverse gear and pulled his prized possessions to the two-room shack in town Biggy shared with his mother and two of his sisters. He brought Biggy his three beat-up ATVs, his TV, and his surround sound. Biggy was dumbstruck. He'd never owned such treasures before.

Then Rasta drove the jeep and empty trailer to Rosie's little farm, just north of the cemetery. He gave Rosie a hug and left her the jeep and trailer, which he knew would be useful hauling feed for the animals. Rosie drove him back to the marina and then waited to give Flo a lift home.

That evening, Rasta and Biggy were sitting on the bench talking for the last time.

"Listen here," Rasta said to his friend, "I had little shares in this place, you know . . . but so did lots of folk."

Night was falling all over the marina, and Rasta could barely make out the rock cliff across the lagoon where he and Bobby were going to build their luxury hotel. He shook his head trying to make sense of the inexplicable.

"Bobby let debts get him . . . Spendin money everywhere. Promisin this one, that one. He sellin part of the marina to different people, fifteen people. Promisin Dennis. Promisin, promisin, you know. Every time he can't pay electric, he promise a part to somebody. And then he make a big promise. He sign a paper. What it matter? Only a paper. Bobby sign anything."

They sat quietly for minutes watching a few sharks cruise listlessly between the pilings. Rasta was leaving the next morning on a twenty-four-foot sailboat brought to the island three days earlier by two friends from Nassau. His friends were big men with dreads like him.

"I put my friends in one of the empty cottages on the beach. Didn't think why not—been no renters for months. But Bobby believe I bring fellas here to hurt him. Can you imagin?"

"I tell em, 'Bobby, you like my brotha. I'll never do nuthin to hurt you. Never in my life. You a part of me. You teach me.' But Bobby don't lisin anymore. He gone to anotha place."

After a pause.

"Bobby turn off all the lights in the house, lock hisself up."

Rasta pointed up the hill from the docks toward Bobby's blackened house.

"They hidin, I tell you."

"Cause of the dog?"

"Marlin made him crazy."

"Can't understan why Dennis do such a thing to Bobby dog."

"Listen here, Biggy. I was right there. Fellas got drunk and put Marlin on top of the new bar. Everyone laughin. And you know, Dennis don't like a dog. He pick up a board and strike Marlin on the head. Marlin fall to the ground, jus whimperin. And Dennis, he pick up a heavy stone and smash him again in the head. Was a gruesome sight. He kick the dog, try to kill Marlin. Dennis gonna throw him off the dock, was when I come over . . . Marlin was Bobby best friend."

"No, you his best friend, Rasta. Built this place."

"Yeah, but um Marlin was Bobby best friend."

"Better than you?"

"Oh yeah. I know the kind of love Bobby have for animals. You know, animals would never betray him. You understan what I sayin? In Bobby life, betrayal be always in the air. He always fightin it. Always makin it happen."

After another pause.

"I carry Marlin up the hill to Bobby who start cryin. Bringing blankets and ice. Holdin Marlin in his arm. Both of them cryin. She love that dog too, tryin to understan things here in this place. Bobby carin for Marlin like mother of a dyin baby."

"I don't see Bobby for days after that. Get to the point where I stop going down to the marina. I had my stuff down there. Bobby was rentin my vehicles, keeping the money for hisself. Mostly I stayin in my bed. I talk to my sister on the phone. She say, 'Rasta, don't stay in that room anymore. Go down there, tell Bobby how you feel.' So I went down the marina. He was carvin outside the office under the almond tree. Tears of rage come into my eyes. I say to him, 'Bobby, I don't like how you treatin me like an outsider. You pushin me outta here. That what you want?'

"While I talkin to him, Bobby has his shades on and he carving a skull, a beautiful skull. I could see tears coming down from under his shades and he say, 'My best friend died last week. And my other friend went against me.'"

~

Three days later.

Hannah sat up in bed at the sound of one of the dogs retching. "Go back to sleep," Bobby said without opening his eyes. It wasn't unusual for one of their dogs to vomit on the worn rug. But she recognized Cisco's whimpering and couldn't sleep. After a while she got out of bed and went into the living room. The dogs were scattered here and there breathing deeply. Cisco smelled of vomit and shit. Hannah sat on the floor and he put his head into her hand, looked up at her gratefully.

Soon after dawn Bobby was up and dressed, heading for the marina. He wasn't concerned about Cisco. His dogs were voracious eaters. "Get him a bucket of water. So he can flush it through. Probably ate some old bait on the dock."

Bobby was now running the whole operation himself. He was hustling from the fuel dock to the office, catching dock lines when the boats came in after fishing, running back to the kitchen. He needed Flo to make salad and keep the kitchen straight, but she was always anxious to get home to her little girl. Flo was in another world. Bobby needed to find someone to replace her, but there wasn't time to look.

Cisco was wobbly all day and by the time Bobby came back after dinner he couldn't stand up. The other three dogs were walking around as if they were drunk and there was bloody diarrhea all over the floor. Mixed into the mess were chewed-up plastic bags. Hannah was moving from one dog to the next, petting, hugging. They were all so sick. Hannah had pots of water set out around the room but none of the dogs were drinking.

One of the homes on the beach was owned by a vet who was off the island. Bobby tried to reach him in Fort Lauderdale, but there was no answer.

He drove his jeep to the tiny island clinic. The block building was dark and locked up. A nurse visited Rum Cay one weekend a month, but a note on the door said she wasn't returning to the island for another three weeks.

Bobby was trying to hold it together. He'd lost Marlin, and now Marlin's babies were all sick, mortally sick. They were his family. Plastic bags. Why plastic bags?

Bobby broke a window at the clinic, looked around inside with his Maglite. He found a cardboard box filled with saline bags and IV hook-ups. He grabbed the stuff and drove back to his house.

All four Labs were lying on the ground, panting and feverish. Blood was coming from their asses and black tar was vomiting from their mouths. The place was rank with mortal disease. Bobby quickly fashioned IV hook-ups from broomsticks and scrap lumber. He'd jury-rigged IV drips before when there was an accident or illness and no doctor or nurse on the island. He knew that each of the saline bags would last about eight hours.

"Bobby, I took rotten vegetables out of the refrigerator. Maybe I left them on the counter."

He shook his head dismissively, began operating like a machine. He was like this whenever an accident occurred in the marina and he needed to stitch up an arm or a belly, or he had to make preparations for a category four hurricane closing on the island. At such times he shifted into another gear and did the work, grim though it might be. He directed his wife to comfort their dogs, coax them to sip water.

He fell into bed a few hours before dawn. Bobby had a marina filled with boats and guests. He needed to push the dogs from his mind, smile, and remain optimistic around his customers.

For the next two days, the dogs held their own. Cisco even started walking again and the others were sipping a little water. Hannah cared for them almost without taking a break. Bobby worked the marina, promising the world while he served them dessert.

When Bobby woke the morning of the fourth day, Hannah was holding Cisco in her arms, crying, and rocking mournfully. The big Lab was dead.

"I left their food outside in bowls rotting in the sun." She spit out the words like poison.

"I killed them, Bobby."

Hannah's despair spilled all over and had no quarter. She was trapped in a loop—the spoiled vegetables on the counter, the dog food rotting in the sun.

"You didn't kill anything. Stop it."

Hannah couldn't stop. She'd poisoned her dogs. Gave away her baby daughter.

"You didn't do this. Stop writing your fucking book."

Bobby's own grief was now sheared by rage. He knew, or thought he knew.

Still, he tried to restrain himself. His marina was crowded with boats. The dreams of his father, from the day he'd discovered this place, had become Bobby's dreams.

By the middle of the afternoon, two of the other Labs

were dead and the fourth was just barely alive. Bobby was on the phone with the vet from Fort Lauderdale. He carefully explained what needed to be done.

"Yeah, I can do it," he said.

Bobby carried Cisco to Rasta's house across the yard. He turned on the naked overhead bulb and then dragged inside a worktable from outside that he occasionally used for sculpting coral. He placed Cisco on the table, spread his legs and cut him down the middle. Evening mosquitoes quickly settled all over Bobby's arms and face while Bobby did the careful work. He cut away Cisco's liver, then his kidneys, his heart, and his stomach. Bobby placed each of the organs, in a separate plastic bag, brushed aside flies and mosquitoes before sealing the bag. The vet explained that none of these body parts could be frozen or it would make the lab work more difficult and maybe even impossible. Bobby put the plastic bags in their refrigerator. The following morning, they were flown off the island.

It was three days before the vet called back to say there were traces of chopped meat in Cisco's stomach along with a cocktail of difethialone and zinc phosphide—enough poison to kill twenty dogs.

Bobby was out the door before Hannah could make sense of it.

No more reflecting or nudging. Bobby went to the back of his house and climbed onto his old excavator, snapped on the powerful headlights. He began steaming down the hill from his property and then headed north on the beach road. If he happened to see Dennis out walking, he'd run him down, then run back and forth across his fat belly. He was thinking this, hoping for the chance while he barreled the big screaming machine several miles toward the north end of the beach. Bobby was going to end it. He wasn't sure how yet. Tonight. He wasn't thinking about tomorrow or the guests at the marina or fueling the fishing boats. Just to kill that fat piece of shit and end it.

~

Dennis owned a palace on the beach, ten thousand square feet of nouveau riche grandeur lit up with banks of floodlights like a small stadium. When Bobby pulled into the driveway, he was center stage. Dennis's Land Rover wasn't in the driveway but beside the front door, and framed on both sides by ornate marble pillars, was a shiny red all-terrain Honda. Bobby lowered the bucket of the excavator and piled into the vehicle and then he flipped it over and smacked into it a couple of more times with the teeth of the bucket. Then he aimed his bucket at Dennis's front door and busted it open, and then he knocked over one of the pillars. It felt like punching Dennis in the gut. No one came out of the house. But several of Dennis's workers who lived in quarters behind the guesthouse came out to investigate. They watched a lunatic at work and knew not to try to stop him.

Bobby looked around, frustrated. He wanted to kill Dennis with his hands. Most likely Dennis was at the marina on his boat or sitting at his bar with a few cronies. Bobby again lowered the bucket of the excavator and began digging a crosshatch of trenches into Dennis's driveway. When he'd made it impassable, he drove off into the night.

~

Soon as Dennis got a phone call at the marina about Bobby's mayhem, he broke into a wide smile—that's what his men recalled, because Dennis rarely smiled, fully smiled. It must have felt as though he had walked through a gate to the promised country. For a long while he'd been sleepwalking, stumbling ahead, but no more. Bobby had been winning the slow game. Bobby had given Dennis the gift he'd been waiting for.

"Bobby's gone crazy," Dennis said to a small crowd gathered around the stern of his boat. "He's a menace to this island. We have to get Bobby. Get him tonight. Before he does something else."

Within fifteen minutes the police sergeant, the only cop on the island, was standing behind Dennis's boat, along with a posse of four men from town. "Bobby's lost his mind," Dennis said to them. "Tried to kill my workers with a backhoe. Now we have to catch him or do whatever's necessary."

The police sergeant was wearing a bulletproof vest and carrying a rifle. Four other men were holding baseball bats.

There were crews and owners from other boats standing around, feeling the peril of the night. Rumors were spreading through the marina. Bobby had gone mad. The police sergeant got on the VHF radio and stuttered the words, "Bobby Little wanted dead or alive."

Even Mike came out of his decaying sailboat to listen and watch. There had never been such a scene like this on the dock—a hunting party for Bobby Little, who was the creator and benevolent if flawed king of the land. It was the first time Mike had been seen on the dock in months. He was pale and gaunt from no sun and living on rice and little else. He was taking in the moment, perhaps taking notes for his novel. Maybe he'd intuited this story line, or already written a version but from knowing him a little I suspect the pace of the story had become unattractive to Mike. There was way too much plot coming at him, plot snuffing out all gradation and reflection. Mike was an author who lingered on the changing nuance of a smile. I suspect the vulgarity of the night, the baseball bats, the crowing of Dennis, was terribly unsettling. After five or ten minutes, Mike nodded at no one in particular and ducked back below.

Although from another perspective, the scene on the dock

might have seemed preposterous and forlorn—all the glory of Bobby's place gone to this ragtag hunting party assembled behind Dennis's boat. "Bobby Little wanted dead or alive," the police sergeant stuttered again and again into the VHF radio. His men, out-of-work fishermen and town drunks, each of them owned by Dennis, were readying themselves beside a nearby palm tree, gripping bats and muttering curses.

"Wanted Dead or Alive" spread through the marina to each of the twenty-five boats. Grand fishing plans for the morning were hastily abandoned. Preparations were made by boaters to leave the island at first light when it would be safe to navigate the reef.

~

With the bucket of the excavator Bobby pushed a few boulders into his narrow driveway, making it difficult for Dennis and his men to follow in their vehicles. He drove the excavator up the hill toward his house, parked it behind a couple of tall trees. He was worried Dennis would burn it up but didn't put much effort into hiding it. For some reason, Bobby felt like he was moving in slow motion.

Hannah was caring for the remaining female Lab that seemed to have gained a little strength. She was feeding her spoons of some kind of soft food and Hannah's expression had turned peaceful, as though she were mothering her baby.

"Come on, we gotta go," he urged.

"Why, Bobby?"

It seemed like too much to explain—too big and impossible to explain. Hannah was in another world, the dog licking her hand, an ethereal expression on her face that made Bobby feel grateful.

"While you were gone, I baked some banana muffins." She gestured to the muffins on the counter.

"Maybe a little later, baby."

Bobby had always been a great finisher but suddenly he felt exhausted, like he'd punched himself out in the third round. Bobby sat on a chair and watched his wife care for the surviving dog. He had an urge to take her hand, to sit beside her in a chair holding hands. He no longer cared about Dennis or the fishing boats in the marina. He wanted to sit a while, breathe the night air as if he were living in an entirely different book.

It wasn't the right moment for such epiphanies. Bobby heard the shriek of a police siren coming from down the hill.

Bobby picked up the dog in his arms and started to pull Hannah out of the house, but she insisted on going back to the counter and putting her muffins in a paper bag.

"Why do we have to rush like this?"

She didn't get it. All of Hannah's demons lived inside her. They walked a hundred yards east to a neighbor's house. Bobby asked if Hannah and their dog could spend the night.

Bobby gave his wife a hug and said he'd call her in a few hours on her cell phone.

"Look, Bobby," she said with an endearing smile. Hannah pointed at the female Lab that was now able to stand and walk a few steps. They could start over again with that dog. She looked at Bobby to say this.

~

Bobby wasn't quite sure what to do next. He would have settled for a draw but that wasn't in the rules.

He sprinted back to his place, grabbed his hunting bow, four arrows, and his satellite phone, threw a couple of bottles of water in a backpack, and stuffed a bandanna in his pocket. He always hunted with a bandanna.

By the time he was outside the house, he could see flashlights aiming up the driveway, four or five men from what he could tell. He could also make out the flashing light of the police car parked at the bottom of the hill. The police sergeant would be carrying a rifle.

They'd be on him in a minute.

Just to the southwest of Bobby's property was a fifty-acre tract of land overgrown with thistles and bush. Bobby bolted into the briar patch. It was his only chance. He'd hunted goats in this rough terrain years earlier and still recalled the dips and ruts and a few paths that were long overgrown with high grass, and hurtful bushes and plants with inviting names like cuttlefish and wild powder puff. Bobby burrowed into it, one arm protecting his face. He could hear the men coming from the road, hear them breathing. He stumbled into a ditch and threw himself onto the ground, trying to cover himself with thorny bushes.

He was lying on his back and could see distorted beams of flashlights passing on both sides of him. His heart was banging in his chest. Could they hear this pounding? One of the men was swinging at trees or rocks with his bat. They were very poor men who had been paid well. They'd come to kill him. It was a sobering moment. There would be no talking or convincing them. He heard the men muttering about the thorny bushes. Bobby had the beginning of an idea. If he could survive.

When the men were no longer close, he started edging his way through the bush, heading west—that's where he wanted to go, but he wasn't really sure where he was going. Must get deeper into this forest where they couldn't find him. Survive. Just trying to survive, until he crawled into one of the overgrown paths. This gave him a little confidence. It was home territory—at least in the daytime it was. He crawled ahead on his hands and knees, getting pricked every time he put his hands down. For a while, maybe twenty minutes, he didn't hear any sounds of men. He felt like he could take a deep breath. *Fuck you, Dennis. I'm still alive.* Bobby continued to crawl ahead until he heard the sound of moving water.

Ten years earlier he and Rasta had built a series of narrow run-off canals from the west end of the lagoon leading to the ocean. Bobby was at a decisive corner in his journey, left into the canal toward the ocean, or straight ahead into the bush where he'd be more difficult to find. *Which way, Bobby? Which way?* He didn't know. Something had changed in Bobby. Something basic he didn't understand. Always he had been a decisive man, but now there was some hesitation. He wasn't sure. As if he'd been infected by her journal of musing and worry. *Which way, Bobby?*

He climbed into the water up to his waist and headed for the ocean. For sure he might have lived the night in the forest of bushes and small trees, but what about the morning? They would get him then. They'd find him in the morning, club him to death, or maybe they'd do something to Hannah. If Bobby was able to kill Dennis, his men would disappear into the village, resume their quiet lives as conch fishermen and handymen, as if there had never been any Dennis with his mega bar and mansion on the beach. They would hail Bobby on the road when he drove by in his jeep as if this moonless night had never happened. If he could somehow kill Dennis.

The canal was also overgrown with bushes and small trees providing perfect cover. He moved more quickly here, confident they wouldn't see him. It was more or less a mile to the ocean. The water was cool and he made the walk without much effort.

Bobby laid on his belly at the top of a sandy bluff looking out across the beach to the dark ocean. To the north Dennis's beach house, lit up like a rock concert. To the south he could see lights on the towers of fishing boats. North or south? Was Dennis at his house or at the marina? No telling, fifty-fifty. Either way Bobby needed to get to the ocean.

But maybe he should have spent the night in the bush, hidden himself, waited a day or two until Dennis and his men grew weary of looking for him. Walking on the beach he'd be out in the open like a trapped rat. Maybe. Maybe.

Bobby walked back to the canal, waded back in, and plunged his hands into the soft muck on the side of the bank and smeared it all over his face and arms. He remembered to put on his bandanna. He went back onto the bluff and looked out across the beach. No one around. Then he made a soundless shriek, sprinted across the beach, and walked into the water.

North or south? Where was Dennis? If he had a coin he might have flipped it. He shook his head and started walking south toward the marina. The warm beach water was about chest high and Bobby held his bow and arrows over his head. He knew better than anyone that on the low tide the bull and tiger sharks from the marina left the lagoon to hunt along the inside reef just twenty or thirty yards offshore from where he was walking, big sharks. He tried not to think about one of them pulling him under. He strained to walk without splashing, which was exhausting. It was about a half mile to the marina. He passed the five unlit guesthouses just north of the fuel depot.

Bobby crawled from the ocean on his belly, pulling the bow behind him on the sand heading for the big diesel tanks that loomed eerily against the dark sky. If any of Dennis's men stepped out onto the beach to have a smoke, there would be no escape. But no one did.

The six rusty five-thousand-gallon tanks were sitting on a concrete slab soaked with leaked diesel fuel. Bobby crawled from one to the next until he was behind a tank closest to the marina dock. He stood for a better view. Most of the fishermen had retired to their boats for the night, but he could see the policeman sitting on the transom of Dennis's boat. A couple of his men were hanging around nearby.

Dennis was seated in the imposing fighting chair of the boat, about a hundred yards from where Bobby was standing. Most of his body was obscured by the hamburger bar, but Bobby could see Dennis's head and shoulders. He watched Dennis take a drink of something from a large red cup. He thought about taking his shot at Dennis's head or neck. Thought about it. Then getting out of there. Calling Hannah. Escaping. *No, no, too far away.* If he missed, the men would chase him down and kill him.

Bobby crawled through the tanks until he was off the slab

onto sandy grass and heading for the tiny laundry room where Flo did the wash. For about fifty feet, he was out in the open. He could hear the men slurring their words. That was good—they were drunk. He made it to the laundry room. Took a few deep breaths.

He was covered in sandy diesel fuel, tried to wipe his hands clean on his shorts. He needed to have dry hands.

Between the laundry room and Bobby's clubhouse, there was a narrow corridor. Bobby slowly crawled between the buildings. He was close to the boats but couldn't see them. Blocking his view was a covey of small palm trees, but he was close.

He crawled ahead toward the dock stinking of diesel fuel and terror. Bobby crawled forward until he was right behind the trees. He stood up, moved the leaves aside, and could see Dennis in his chair, his piggish squinting eyes. Again he wiped his right hand, this time on his bandanna. Dennis said a few words to the policeman. The bar was a few feet off to Bobby's right. A clear shot. They were all drunk. Dennis was holding the sippy cup in his left hand.

Bobby's shot was now about forty yards. This was about as close as he would be able to get. Bobby kept shifting his position, a foot here and there to find a crack in the palm leaves. He'd only have one shot at this. No, they kept snapping back in front of his face. No open spaces to take a shot from behind the trees.

Only one way. Bobby notched his arrow. Took four or five deep breaths and quietly walked out of the trees holding the bow. He was standing in the open now, clear as day.

Bobby drew down on Dennis in the chair, aiming for his chest, reminded himself to relax the fingers of his right hand, was about to let it go when the police sergeant passed in front of the chair.

Hold it, Bobby. Hold it. Hold it.

Bobby, standing alone in the yard like a statue, held the sixty-pound bow at full draw for about a half minute until he again had a clear shot at center chest, took notice of Dennis's fat supercilious expression. Then, a moment seemingly devoid of all thought, all sense, Bobby's archer's eye fell on the sippy cup sitting in the holder just to the left of Dennis's belly. Changed his aim just slightly, pulled the barb of the arrow firmly against the bow, relaxed the fingers again, and he let it go.

Dennis ducked and screamed like he'd been hit. The arrow had pierced the center of the cup and lodged in the mahogany door to Dennis's salon. Everyone on the boat turned to look at the arrow. When they turned around, Bobby was gone.

~

Before dawn, Biggy came for Hannah. He led her through hidden paths in the small forest until they arrived at the salt pond, as Bobby had instructed him on the satellite phone. Biggy knew this terrain even better than Bobby. During hot summer days, when the shallow lake water evaporated, Biggy came here to collect salt off the bottom with a wooden rake. He made a few dollars selling three-pound bags of Bahamian sea salt to wives visiting the marina on fishing boats.

Bobby was waiting for them seated on a rock, covered in mud and diesel fuel. Hannah began to laugh at the sight and then caught herself.

"Why'd you leave me like that—without even a word?"

He shook his head. "How was your night, baby?"

"You can't do that to me, Bobby. I couldn't sleep two hours with that dog licking my hand. I'm exhausted and all pricked up from that walk."

"I'm sorry, baby."

She leaned over to give him a kiss.

"Phew. You smell like gasoline."

"Diesel fuel."

"Oh, diesel fuel."

Just then the small seaplane banked in from the southwest and landed at the far side of the lake. Bobby glanced at the plane idling toward them but mostly he was scanning the tree line.

Why was his pilot buddy, Grover, coming ahead so goddamned slowly? Bobby had a knot in his belly, watching the trees for the police sergeant and his goons to race in on them with baseball bats.

He smirked a little, thinking, he could have shot Dennis in the chest last night and ended it. Now it might never end.

"You must be starved," she said.

Hannah held the muffin in front of him, so he wouldn't have to touch it, and Bobby took famished bites.

"Can we come up here sometimes? It's beautiful here." She was looking at two egrets standing in the shallow water searching for crustaceans.

"Sure we can."

Bobby looked at the tree line. Took Hannah's hand and pulled her to the plane that had just eased up to them, pushed her into the back seat.

Grover didn't even bother to ask, just moved over into the passenger seat. Bobby always did the piloting when he flew with Grover.

Before setting the autopilot to Nassau, Bobby headed the small plane back toward the marina. He came in low, passed over the docks, and could see a few men standing behind Dennis's boat. All the other fishing boats had left the marina. The police car was parked nearby. Dennis was assembling his men.

Bobby couldn't resist, circled back again, came in even lower, and this time he dipped the wing on his side so the men in the stern of Dennis's boat would see him leaning out the window, offering a thumbs up.

~

Seven days later, Bobby and Hannah were flying back to Rum Cay in another seaplane. For this flight, Bobby sat in the copilot seat, Hannah was in the back beside a tall black man about fifty. She was writing in her journal. Bobby was looking down at the choppy ocean just north of Conception Island. He hadn't seen a single boat headed in the direction of Rum Cay. Not one boat. Just open ocean. Senator Charles Saunders was piloting his own plane.

For the past week Bobby and Hannah had stayed at a small resort on Paradise Island. On their first day in Nassau, Bobby had made a phone call to an old marina client from years earlier, Charles Saunders, an attorney and presently a member of the Senate, an appointee of the prime minister. The following day they met in Saunders's law office and Bobby described recent dire events on the island and how he'd been lucky to get off Rum Cay alive. Saunders listened trying to reconcile this unsettling story with his own pleasant memories of the marina. Finally, he said he wanted to see all this for himself.

Saunders offered to fly Bobby back to Rum Cay in his own plane. He suggested they should bring along a private detective he knew from Miami, a man who couldn't be bought off and would know how to research Dennis's mysterious Rum Cay real estate titles and building permits as well as his financial transactions with the local policeman and others on the island. Once they had this information, they could begin legal proceedings. And just in case, the retired detective would be carrying a handgun.

Returning with the renowned senator made Bobby feel like the battle was already won. The police sergeant would cower and stutter searching for excuses, or he would try to hide in the village. Just a little mopping up, and life would return to normal. Bobby began thinking about his business, how many boats would be tied up at the dock when they got there, how many reservations had come in for the following months. He yawned, his mind going to his restaurant. He needed help there, for sure. He couldn't get Flo to do a thing. He needed to find a few good people to work for him. Maybe if he called Rasta, he could talk him into coming back and helping. Why the hell had he fallen out with Rasta? Bobby could no longer summon a trace of the anger. *Why do such things happen?* He should have listened to his wife.

He fell asleep thinking about Hannah. They were so different, but she made him feel alive. Hannah understood sorrows and delights he had never slowed down to notice. Bobby had messed up so many relationships and marriages. He didn't want to spoil things with her. He'd build the little arts and crafts store down by the dock where she could sell her books and other lovely island things. *Why not?*

~

The light seaplane came down hard in the choppy bay, skipped a couple of times, and threw water onto the windshield. Bobby thought the rough landing was part of a dream. He wiped his eyes, disoriented. The windshield was obscured with seawater. Bobby blinked a couple of times, bent over the senator to look out his side window.

"Where are we?" he asked.

"Wake up, fella. Where do you think you are?"

Now Bobby could see out the windshield. Just to the south he saw the big diesel tanks. But when he looked to his left, he felt confused.

"Really, where are we?"

"Wake up, Bobby. You're home."

"No, really, we're not."

They anchored the plane in two feet of water, right off the beach, not far from where Bobby had crawled ashore with his bow and arrow eight days earlier.

"Where are my fucking guesthouses?"

There weren't any guesthouses overlooking the beach. Bobby rubbed his eyes again. No guesthouses but instead there were high mounds of sand and some ruts and deep tracks.

"What the hell?"

The four of them crossed the beach to the bluff and then walked south until they reached the concrete slab with the fuel tanks.

From here they had a perfect view of the marina or rather a view of where the marina should have been.

"Oh my," said Hannah.

It was gone. The marina was gone. There was no more clubhouse and dining room. No more hamburger bar. The laundry house had vanished. The fuel dock and the office, the surfboard shack had disappeared as well as most of the slips for the fishing boats. All the docks and slips were gone except for an eight- or ten-foot section of the old dock where Mike's aged sailboat was tied up. There were no other boats in the placid harbor. There wasn't a single standing structure.

They walked the property taking in the mounds of sand, the emptiness. All of Bobby's sculptures had disappeared, although here and there they saw shards of coral, a part of a barracuda tail, a turtle flipper, the shattered head of Neptune.

Then, as they rounded the bend on the narrow sand path heading toward town, they could see one tiny building still remained. The shed where Bobby and Rasta did their sculpting in the afternoon was still standing, the soiled canvas door flapping in the breeze. It was the only remaining structure on the property.

Bobby understood almost immediately. If Dennis couldn't have the marina, no one would. He knew that Bobby would return to the island bringing help. Dennis came with his large bulldozer and two excavators and knocked it all down. Dennis and his crew tore down forty years of work in one day and then pushed it all into the sea.

Bobby was remembering, smiling. Forty years ago he had come here from Miami as a spindly seven-year-old. He was a misfit in school, a cutup and troublemaker, always feeling badgered and hemmed in. He got into fights and couldn't bear sitting in class. Bobby's mom and dad had been standing about where the diesel tanks were now, discussing this remote place and their dream of building a little marina in the midst of the vast ocean.

Young Bobby had looked down the expanse of virgin beach to the north and noticed a black stingray skimming just beneath the rippling waves. He started following the giant sea creature, jogging on the beach. He kept running along the sand, faster and faster to keep up with the creature. A little boy running with his arms flailing toward the emptiness and beauty of this place where the ocean reached the sky, nothing here at all and yet there was so much.

Hannah seemed to get it without a word. Bobby appraised his wife and nodded a couple of times.

~

In the evening, the four of them, and the female Lab, Cleo, walked back down the hill from Bobby's house to the empty harbor and over to the tiny slab of dock where Mike's sailboat was tied up, seemingly for all eternity just as Bobby had promised Mike. Biggy was now sitting on the dock where he'd often met Rasta for talks about life. He came here most afternoons to meet the boats, hoping to find a girl he could love. Dreams die very hard.

Rasta's little friend affirmed everything Bobby had surmised. Dennis had come to the marina with his heavy equipment and wrecked the place in one day.

Then he reported another surprise.

A few days later, some kids had been playing on the road, near Bobby's little sculpture studio. They heard some town dogs barking and watched them running in and out of the canvas door to the shack that was buzzing with flies. One of the kids went over and pulled aside the soiled canvas and saw a fat man lying on his belly on top of broken pieces of coral and cutting and grinding tools. Dennis lay on the ground with his throat cut and his shorts pulled down to his knees. His legs had been partially eaten by the hungry dogs.

The kids ran for their lives.

The police sergeant called in detectives from Nassau who flew into Rum Cay to investigate. Two detectives questioned every soul on the island. Bobby was an obvious suspect but he was off the island. Rasta had left weeks earlier. The detectives could find no murder weapon, no witness, no clues at all. After two days the detectives were called back to Nassau where there were murders to investigate every day.

Epilogue

The crew of the *Ebb Tide* woke to a rare windless morning with the surface of Port Nelson Bay so glossy it functioned like the lens of a gigantic magnifying glass. Except for Jim, who was limping more than usual, we climbed to the bridge to take in the view. Every triggerfish, strawberry grouper, jack, or craw-fish meandering below was not just clearly visible but greatly enlarged as though you could take the creature into your hands. In every direction the clear shallow bay was busy with schools of cruising fish, stingrays, a few small sharks on the prowl. I noticed a five-foot barracuda idling behind our transom, flexing its jaws while waiting for us to toss scraps of breakfast. Watching this close-up panorama of life beneath was a little dizzying and after a few minutes I needed to turn away and get my bearings.

In the morning light, it was clear that coral heads between us and the ocean had considerable distances between them and many were deep enough to pass over—our fears coming in the previous night were for the most part ill founded. The bay itself was lovely, a perfect anchorage except for a little surge from the ocean.

But the shore told a different story. The lush green island I knew so well was colored a muddy brown. Most of the palm trees were broken in half and what trees and bushes remained upright were shorn of vegetation, hardly more than branches and sticks. I didn't see anyone standing on the beach or walking on the sand road that runs parallel to the beach.

We passed the binoculars back and forth, focused on the town cemetery by the beach about two hundred feet north of the broken town dock. Many headstones were toppled over, and mixed in with them were bones of the dead, forearms, skulls, thigh bones, ribs. Some bones were corkscrewed into the ground as if there had been a mysterious religious rite. It occurred to me that this desecration was payback for what happened years earlier, when the local people would not allow the Haitians to be buried here. The residents had not buried the bones again whether out of fear or laziness. The sight of scattered bones didn't inspire our appetite for scrambled eggs.

But we did eat some breakfast. Then I heard the raspy sound of an old outboard.

It was Biggy steering an old Boston Whaler our way. He came racing up to us way too fast, shouting greetings and waving exuberantly. Doron called to him to slow down, but

Biggy, excited to see us, forgot to throttle down the outboard. His bow rammed the *Ebb Tide* so hard, Biggy flipped off the stern into the bay.

He came to the surface thrashing, petrified of sharks, shouting, "Get me out, get me outa here."

Jimmy Rolle was doubled over, laughing at the sight, and frankly it was a joy to see him laugh after he'd been so sullen the long trip here from Bimini. Finally, Jim managed to quiet himself, reached over the side and with one powerful arm he pulled Biggy into the *Ebb Tide* like a small marlin.

Biggy put us ashore near the town dock. While we walked the hot sand road to Bobby's house, Biggy described the recent hurricane, every single house and building knocked down except for the church, palm trees, and electric poles snapped like pencils and many graves washed from the earth by flood waters. All but forty residents had abandoned Rum Cay to live on other islands.

When we neared Bobby's steep driveway, Biggy darkened like an eclipse. "Bobby care only about Bobby." He gestured for us to walk up the hill by ourselves and he turned back to the beach.

~

Bobby's house and yard were obscured by a hundred goats pushing and shoving to gulp slop from a few troughs and pots set around the yard while getting nipped and barked at by Bobby's new brood of four big Lab puppies, the progeny of Cleo. The goats sounded like a chorus of frantic babies pleading for help. There were animals everywhere—chickens sprinting out of bushes, hundreds of chickens, cats preparing to pounce, huge pigs laying on the dirt, big dogs barking and jumping all over us.

When the herd shifted, we spotted Bobby Little squatting in a pool of muddy water. The lord of Rum Cay was sponging down a four-hundred-pound pig and smiling like he'd found true bliss; although, it occurred to me that the theater of this moment did not escape him. He climbed out of the mud pond and hosed himself down.

In their roomy kitchen, Hannah was taking a wonderful-smelling banana bread from the oven. There were dogs and goats inside the house as well, but clearly they kept many more outside for our benefit. John began making drawings of their lives in the stone house crowded with needy animals.

"When she came to Rum Cay, we were living on the edge of war," Bobby said, taking a piece of hot bread, "You could almost hear the tanks rolling past. We were in the trenches trying to survive. Finally the walls came down, and we had to retreat to a new zone. But there wasn't a moment to catch our breath."

Soon after the destruction of the marina, a powerful tropical cyclone, Hurricane Joaquin, battered Rum Cay for twenty-four hours. Bobby had constructed a staunch hurricane shelter for their chickens. They bedded down the goats and their dog in the kitchen and living room of the house to survive the storm. But when the hurricane's full force winds of more than 150 miles per hour hit the island, the stone house started to shake and the roof of the kitchen blew off. Bobby and Hannah were afraid the entire house would soon fly into the sea.

When the eye of the storm passed directly over the island and the wind quieted, they gathered their dog and eighteen goats and led them on a Noah's ark half-mile trek along the rough-hewn rim of the cliff. There was no vegetation left on the path to distract the goats, not a green leaf anywhere to eat, so the long trail of animals followed while Bobby and Hannah shook cans of feed to keep their attention. About a half mile from the house, there was a narrow path leading down the rock wall into a deep cave. Bobby knew that if the backside of the storm ramped up before they reached the entrance to the cave they would all be blown into the harbor. But they made it inside safely. The cave had a narrow entrance, but inside it widened at the back end and there were several stone slabs flat enough to sleep on. Hannah and Bobby bedded down with their animals for the next twelve hours while the backside of the hurricane tore over the island destroying virtually everything that was still standing.

"After the storms passed, I needed to put this place back together," he said, "to build safe enclosures for the animals

so they wouldn't wander off. There was so much to learn. I was the guy who'd created the 'Bobby Show,'" he reflected. "Neither of us were farmers. Hannah studied blogs at night, learned how to make mulch piles and bins. How to care for our goats and chickens. What to feed them."

"The goats are our babies," Hannah added. "They are Eddie, Alfred, and Bam Bam. I clean their poops and wipe milk off their faces. Soon as they're born, they move into the house with us and the dogs. There's always new babies arriving. In a year and a half since the hurricane, our herd has grown to more than a hundred."

"Rain is coming tonight," she said a few minutes later. Hannah was being polite, lingering with the guests for a few minutes while waiting for the first civil opportunity to rush off to her animals.

Bobby was ready to talk all afternoon about Rasta and Dennis and the loss of the marina, pointing to ironies and tragedies in the saga with literary panache. "As it turns out, I don't need the glamour, the women, and fancy cars. This foul smelling house of animals is the dream beneath the dream."

But Hannah felt pressured to fix the roof of the Flamingo Inn, a shack she'd built and painted blue with a large pink flamingo on the door, so the goats would have a dry place to spend the rainy night. Then she'd go to the beach and haul heavy sacks of seaweed up the driveway to make fresh bedding for the goats and pigs.

Living up here on the hill, mostly unobserved except by the animals, they'd both been liberated to jettison old baggage. Hannah discovered heartiness in herself she never would have imagined. Apparently, she'd left behind old demons as well as ambitions she flirted with in college but never fully embraced. Her many farm babies were more compelling than a journal of ideas and regrets although she often posted entries on Facebook about the births of goats and puppies. The farm became her art.

Bobby had mellowed, become more reflective. This was my impression.

He did farm chores in the morning and afternoons he made coral sculpture on the outdoor table set out on the bluff with a view of the ocean. For the first time in his life, he didn't feel pressured to rush to the dock to catch lines from fishing boats entering the marina, or to the kitchen to make dinner.

~

Three days before Dennis made his untimely exit from this narrative, and on the very morning he ordered his men to bulldoze Bobby's marina into the ocean, Dennis first invited local residents to come onto the property and empty Bobby's buildings and guest houses, bust out windows and doors, take everything that wasn't cemented in place. Unusual generosity or a deeper form of malice? It's difficult to say.

"Today, when I walk around the village I see the fans

and artwork they took from my guest cottages," Bobby told us while we walked down the hill to the remains of his marina. "After the hurricane, when they rebuilt their houses, they used my stuff they'd squirreled away, my tables, my chairs, silverware, plates, paintings, even some of my sculptures. Everything you can imagine is spread throughout this island. My dive and fishing gear, generators, water makers, everything we worked our whole lives for. It's still here but it's tucked away in their houses. . . . When the town guys are hungry, they sneak up the hill in the night, take a chicken or a goat from our farm. Last week they took two of our pigs."

He shrugged. *That's the way life is here.*

~

The marina had returned to nothing. Just piles of shifting sand, the wind through the rigging of a forgotten sailboat.

We walked around taking in the silence. No more buildings or pretty houses, no signs of the party. Sand dunes and a few memories unimpeded by the hustle of the docks, the promise of lusty pleasures.

We walked to the ocean, feeling the soft sea air, a perfect afternoon for trolling the corner.

Then I noticed that the entrance to the harbor had disappeared. The blast of three hurricanes had filled the channel with dunes of sand, just the way Bobby's parents discovered the place forty years ago.

The marina was now a small man-made lake with the masts of a few sunken sailboats breaking the surface. Only one tiny section of wobbly dock remained. Tied up with crusty lines was an ancient sailboat.

I walked down to the boat and called out, "Mike, Mike." I banged on the old hull. I really had no idea.

After a minute, an old salt looked out his hatch squinting as though he hadn't seen the sun in months. I couldn't believe my eyes. Still here. All these years. Mike had survived three massive hurricanes in his boat. He'd witnessed the whole rise and fall of Bobby's kingdom firsthand. I thought about disturbing and memorable sections of his book he'd read to me years earlier. I wondered if he'd written the last of it from the purgatory of this ghost marina. I hoped I could coax him to show me some recent pages.

We chatted a little about pedestrian things. News in the States. His difficulty getting food. I told him that I had some fresh mahi-mahi on board and I would bring it to him. This pleased him greatly.

Then when I asked about the novel, he told me that two years earlier the hard drive on his computer began to falter and he transferred his files to a thumb drive. Then one day it broke. He could no longer access his pages. They were gone, twelve years of work.

I couldn't believe this news. I felt so bad for him. But Mike had a different take. He was trying to fix the thumb drive and believed that one day it would work again and he'd have his book back. I tried to persuade him to allow me to bring the drive to the States and see if I could have the material salvaged by a professional, but he graciously declined. He was going to work on it himself like repairing an old fishing reel. Maybe he'd retrieve it and maybe he wouldn't. Either way, Mike saw no tragedy here. He was a hermit living in a graveyard of dreams. A novel didn't seem so important.

Before we headed back to the *Ebb Tide*, Jimmy Rolle remarked to Bobby that he could clear his channel in two days of work. "Really, nuthin to it with an excavator."

Bobby nodded and turned away. He knew this, of course. Bobby understood that opening up the channel was an easy job. And after that, the boats would come back to Rum Cay and friends of his would offer to put up the money to fix the docks.

But then, the "Bobby Show" would begin all over again.

~

The following morning, while the other guys slept late, Jim and I were sitting in the salon of the *Ebb Tide*, sipping tea and considering the options. I was wondering if I would ever return to this island that had intoxicated my dreams since I was a young man. Probably not.

I had the feeling the Bobby story had deeply affected my friend Jim. Long ago, he had also been the king of an island. Now he spent days sitting on a milk crate, looking at the dusty road outside an empty grocery store. That's a lot to hold in your head.

In the past, I'd made a few suggestions to Jim about how he and his wife might import a few new products into their tiny store, improve their prospects, but Jim had no heart for this talk. His knees were hurting and mostly he just wanted to sit under his bougainvillea tree beside the store.

"You look good at the road, you can tell a lot," he said. "Just watchin way people movin past."

The salon door of the *Ebb Tide* was open, and we could hear the wind coming off the island and whistling through our outriggers. If the southerly wind held for a few days, we'd have a comfortable following sea all the way back to Bimini to drop off Jim before heading to Florida.

"Maybe things would be better for you if you had a bike," I offered. "You could get around more easily."

"A couple months ago I was thinkin bout a bike," Jim said.

"You mean to buy one?"

"Yeah, but then the idea went away from me."

"Why, Jim?"

"The weather good, I just enjoy sittin on the crate, watchin."

Then I heard a woman's voice carried on the wind.

We both went outside and climbed to the bridge of the old

boat. We looked to the shore and couldn't see a soul, but I heard her, a voice I knew so well that gathered the tragedy and beauty into each phrase. Flo was singing "God Bless the Child."

"You hear her, Jim?"

Acknowledgments

Bobby Little, you were the inspiration for *Deep Water Blues*. Thank you so much for helping me imagine this uncanny story.

I could not have written this without Bonnie and Josh. Josh first urged me to write the saga of Rum Cay fifteen years ago. I started and stopped a half dozen times but wasn't able to break into the mayhem and blood lust of the story. Josh listened patiently to my plaints and then said, just write the novel, Dad. Josh has been a lighthouse in my writing life, no, in my life.

Bonnie has been an inspiring and tireless collaborator in everything I've ever written. She's passed on her break-through ideas and fixed my sentences. She knows my drafts better than I do myself. I probably never would have completed a single book were it not for her urging, her revisions, her saintly patience, her ideas, and her love.

John Mitchell traveled with me on the *Ebb Tide* and

brought the narrative to life with his wonderful drawings. He read drafts of the novel and made important suggestions.

Doron Katzman and James Rolle were key members of my amazing crew of oldies. What great guys they are! What amazing times we shared!

Thank you, Rasta, for allowing me to use your incomparable voice.

Thank you, Paul Slavin and Jon Fine, for giving me thoughtful advice and bringing *Deep Water Blues* into the publishing world.

Thank you, Fauzia Burke, Jeff Umbro, and Joseph Hannon.

Antonia Meltzoff, you are one of the best readers I have ever known.

My dear departed Paul Pines. You were so terribly ill but summoned the energy to weigh in brilliantly on the ending of my little book. So much love to you, dear friend.

Thank you, Alex Twersky, for urging me to write a screenplay—a lot of what I learned from writing a movie went into this little novel.

Jay Bergen, your guidance and counsel was hugely important and I cannot thank you enough.

Thank you, Gabriel Byrne. You are such a deep soul. Your kind words about my little book mean a lot.

Aiden Slavin, it is always such a pleasure to wander with you through the pleasures of books and life. Our discussions of this manuscript were so useful and moving to me.

Chris Clemans, thank you for your smart advice. John Clemans, thanks for your enthusiastic reading, old buddy.

Jack, you were my model for young Bobby coming to Rum Cay for the first time. Our Sunday talks have been so inspiring.

Fred Waitzkin was born in Cambridge, Massachusetts, in 1943. When he was a teenager he wavered between wanting to spend his life as a fisherman, Afro Cuban drummer, or novelist. He went to Kenyon College and did graduate study at New York University. His work has appeared in *Esquire, New York* magazine, the *New York Times Sunday Magazine,* the *New York Times Book Review, Outside, Sports Illustrated, Forbes,* the *Huffington Post,* and the *Daily Beast,* among other publications. His memoir, *Searching for Bobby Fischer,* was made into a major motion picture released in 1993. His other books are *Mortal Games, The Last Marlin,* and *The Dream Merchant.* Recently, he has completed an original screenplay, *The Rave.* Waitzkin lives in Manhattan with his wife, Bonnie, and has two children, Josh and Katya, and two grandsons, Jack and Charlie. He spends as much time as possible on the bridge of his old boat, the *Ebb Tide,* trolling baits off distant islands with his family.

John Mitchell, born 1971 in Southern Illinois, is an American artist. As a draftsman, printmaker, and painter, Mitchell works from direct observation of people, places, and things. He was educated at The School of the Art Institute of Chicago and Yale University. Mitchell lives in Williamsburg, Brooklyn.

FRED WAITZKIN

FROM OPEN ROAD MEDIA

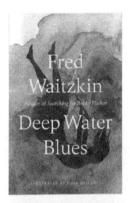

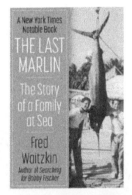

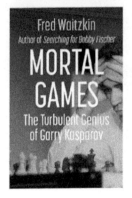

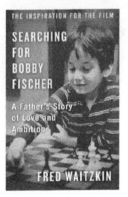

OPEN ROAD

INTEGRATED MEDIA

Find a full list of our authors and
titles at www.openroadmedia.com

FOLLOW US
@OpenRoadMedia

CPSIA information can be obtained
at www.ICGtesting.com
Printed in the USA
BVHW030014110519
548022BV00002B/5/P